Haniah
AND THE
GOLDEN GEM

JASON FORD

ISBN 978-1-942298-45-8

www.snowypeaksmedia.com

For my sweet Hannah, whose bubbly enthusiasm and kind heart has been my inspiration.

NORTH KINGDOM
EAST KINGDOM
STORM SEA
West Kingdom
Mountains of Hayud
Shahirah Forest
West Hills of Aini
Gathbiyya
Desert Canyons of Hafiz
Sirah
White
Kifah
Shadan
Saja
Malak pass
Forest road
Gold road
South road
Coast road
Luja crossing
Stone bridge
Well of Aini
here lies the blue gem high up in the mountains
here lies the red gem in the desert of hafiz light and
here lies the heart of shahrira where the green gem lies in wait of the day in peace and harmony. may your travels be light.
THREE Days Journey

To the Golden Gem it is given
White to light the way in darkness
Blue to soothe the soul in time of sadness
Green to grow courage true
Red to burn the hearts anew

CHAPTER 1

A Royal Crown

Fox-tailed reeds swayed in the summer breeze as Haniah sat on a boulder protruding over the pond near her family's farm. Her bare feet soaked in the warmth from the sun beating overhead. Humming a delightful melody, Haniah braided the long stems of a handful of daisies together, her fingers nimble and skilled from the many hours she had spent mending her own clothing. Holding up the long chain of daisies, she took the ends and wove them together to make a loop.

Haniah placed a hand on the boulder to help herself to her feet. She looked out over the pond and rolling fields to the flock of grazing sheep. Their heads were lowered, chewing on tufts of grass.

Haniah lifted the beautiful loop above her and slowly placed the crown of flowers upon her head. She favored the flock of sheep with a smile, transforming them from grass-eating farm animals to royal court subjects.

All subjects in the court cheered with excitement. Having never seen royalty, Haniah did her best impression of a regal queen. She straightened her back, raised her chin, and imagined she wore an elegant, red dress made of shimmering fabric. On bare toes she twirled about, fanning out her imaginary dress as she spun. Upon her head of curly brown hair sat a radiant crown of gold in place of her newly made daisy wreath. Her castle stood tall around her, with white ramparts that reached to the sky.

In the courtyard, a knight in glistening armor rode a painted horse and raised his hand to salute her.

She lifted her hand in return, but blinked as the mirage faded in front of her. If only her real life was more like the adventurous characters in her books, on which she based her imaginative play. How wonderful life would be! The books her father bought from the peddler once or twice a season were always a delight. Each season, she would anticipate her father coming up the Southern Path. He was sure to bring with him a tale of adventure within the pages of a bound manuscript.

Haniah sighed and plopped back down on the boulder. Instead of living a life of royalty, she was stuck here doing chores from sun up til sun down.

"Chores? Oh dear, I forgot!" she exclaimed.

Haniah looked up at the sun. It would be getting dark in a couple of hours. Her father would be getting home soon.

Haniah hastily picked up her shoes, jumped off the boulder, and was at a sprint by the time her feet hit the trail. The path ran through a grove of whisper oak and feather leaf trees, peppered with lush, rural meadows. Running in full stride, she leapt over a protruding root that grew across the trail. She bounded over rolling hills and passed by the occasional wood squirrel. The pond was not a great distance from home, but far enough to be winded by the time she reached the farm.

Rounding the corner to her home, she saw her father make his way up the Southern Path that led from the town called Stone Bridge. Haniah knew her father had traveled the day's journey on that meandering trail, most likely starting before the sun broke over the horizon, making his way back to the grounds of their well-maintained, quaint farm.

He pulled a fully laden handcart covered with canvas.

Haniah ran to her father, throwing herself against him.

He let go of the cart with one hand and hugged his daughter.

"Father!" cried Haniah. She pulled back and looked up into his eyes. He had a gallant face, with blue, steely eyes and a trimmed beard. He smiled down at her.

"Did you bring me a new book?" she asked.

"I didn't," he said, biting his bottom lip and patting her on the shoulder.

"Did you not see the peddler?"

"I did." His shoulders drooped.

"Did he not have any books to sell?"

"He did, but I did not have the money to buy them." Placing the front of the handcart down on the ground, he turned and looked back at the canvas-covered pile in the cart.

Haniah had noticed the pile before, but this time she really looked. The pile looked just like the pile she saw leaving the farm a few days earlier. Haniah wrinkled her forehead in confusion. "You brought back the wool?" Sitting under the tarp was the wool her father had sheared from their flock of sheep. He had taken it to Stone Bridge to be sold.

"I wasn't able to sell it. No one was buying," he said.

"But why?"

Her father frowned contemplatively. "It seems to me the town folk were not wanting to buy what we had to offer."

To the young girl this news was bewildering. Each summer, her father would shear the sheep and take the wool to town to sell. With the earnings, he would purchase supplies and tools before returning to the farm. She could also expect a new book or something sweet for her and her brother, for being well-behaved children as he put it. It had been that way for as long as she could remember. The goods purchased from Stone Bridge were used to ensure they got through the season. As sad as she felt to know that she was not going to have a new adventure to read and daydream upon, it was clear her father was just as disappointed. The weight of carrying back a full load was apparent in his creased forehead and slumped shoulders.

"Were you able to buy tools and seed?" asked Haniah.

"No," he spoke softly.

"What are we going to do?"

"Well, for starters, I'll put the wool back in the barn. We can use it to spin and we will make yarn from it. You and your mother can sew clothing and see if we can sell that later in the summer. Maybe by that time we can make new negotiations." Careful not to mess with her crown of flowers, he gently placed his hand on her head and lightly tousled her curly brown hair.

"You know," he said smiling, "I always wanted a daughter with curly brown hair. Just like your mother's."

She smiled up at him sheepishly. "I know," she said.

He pulled her close. "I know it's disappointing not to get a new story. But I promise you, your situation will not last forever. As soon as we can, I will make the trip and try again." He looked at her for a moment before continuing. "I am glad to be home. I missed you." He let go of her and spoke again. "I have to speak with your mother. Have you done your chores yet?"

"No, not yet. I was just on my way to milk Antoinette."

Before her father could say his next word, a cool breeze washed over the fields from the West. Haniah felt as though she had been doused with a chilled bucket of water. Small bumps formed on her skin. Her father paused to listen to the rustling leaves and took a deep breath to smell the air.

"What is it, Father?"

"There is something on the wind," replied her father. He had always had extraordinary senses. He could smell the faintest flower scent in the breeze. He could see distant goats on a mountain, even when the mountain could scarcely be seen by ordinary eyes.

"Is it wolves?" asked Haniah.

"I am not sure what it is." He looked back over his shoulder toward the Southern Path and then back at her. "I want you to get the cow in the shed and finish up your chores." He was no longer smiling. "Don't forget to bring in water for washing up this evening. I am going to go bring the sheep in tonight. Do you know where they are?"

"I saw them in the meadows by the pond."

Leaving his daughter and the cart full of wool behind, he walked up the hill from the path where they had greeted one another. Haniah stood where she was, watching his lengthy stride as he passed out of sight.

She turned and made her way to the clearing. On one side of the clearing stood a thatched-roof, two-story cottage with iron-paned windows and a large vegetable garden growing next to it. The windows were washed and decorated with colorful curtains. The door was painted a beautiful forest green with a light yellow trim. On the other side of the clearing stood a barn, slightly larger than the cottage. It was not as charming or cozy, but served its purpose by providing shelter for the animals on the farm.

Two hens pecked the ground in the clearing as she walked to the barn and the gate behind it. Beyond the gate was a small pasture with one brown and white spotted milk cow.

"Come on, Queen Antoinette. It's time for your milking." Haniah picked up the leash attached to the cow's bridle. She was ten summers old and had been given the chore of taking care of the cow for as long as she could remember.

The cow looked up from her grazing and lazily followed Haniah into the barn. She absently guided the cow, thinking instead about how her father's disposition had changed when the wind came. Something was in the wind. It could be wolves. They started having trouble with wolves about a season earlier. The wolves had shown up in the hills last summer, and that's when things had begun to change. First they ate the wildlife, and Father often came back from hunts without seeing a single deer or rabbit. Soon the wolves turned to easier prey like their sheep.

Along with the wolves, the winter months had been especially hard. The bitter cold sunk deep into the ground, and the family had used up all their food stores to feed themselves. The need to replenish the farm's supplies made selling the wool in town all the more important.

But the wolves and cold weather were not the most troubling events. The nights had become longer and the moon dimmed, refusing to shine its reflective light upon the world. Then there were the stars. They had faded away into an inky black sky over the last few months until they shone no more.

These occurrences brought serious concern to the girl's thoughts for the first time in her life. She knew the events also worried her father. She had overheard him speaking with her mother about the darkness one day. They stopped their conversation when she had walked into the room. And just the other night she saw him staring up at the night sky, maybe looking for a glimmer of light.

"If it *is* the wolves, I am sure father will take care of it." She spoke to Antoinette as if the cow would have concerns similar to her own.

She walked the cow to a stall, placed a wooden pail under the cow and squatted beside it on a three-legged stool. There, she began milking. Slowly the pail began to fill with white, creamy milk. Twice a day, morning and evening, Antoinette was milked. Haniah attended to the cow so regularly that she often referred to her as Queen Antoinette. The cow was like a demanding ruler, always in need of her services, always needing milking. "I'll tell you, Antoinette, when I am queen, I will not be as demanding as you. I can think of a hundred things I would rather be doing right now."

Antoinette turned her head toward the girl, wagged her tail in response and returned her attention to the feed bag.

"I mean, if I were queen, I would hope the people were off playing and enjoying the sun. I wouldn't stick them in a stall and expect them to work all the time. I would be a wonderful ruler. I would shower the people with all their desires." She paused from milking and patted a brown patch on the cow's flank. "Well? What do you think? Would I be a good ruler or not?"

The cow chewed the feed in response.

"Goes to show how much help you are," she said as she removed the flower ring from her head and set it on a wood post.

The barn door opened and in skipped a small figure wearing well-trimmed overalls. The boy, wearing a light blue shirt with his sleeves rolled up, used his thin arms to pull himself up on a cask next to the girl milking the cow. His happy grin spread from ear to ear. Upon his head was a mop of wavy brown locks. Unlike his hair, his face was clean and well-kept, like his clothing. "Mother wants to know if you have the milk. She says she is going to make a cake and will need it soon." His grin, impossibly, seemed to grow bigger with his declaration of cake.

"What kind of cake?" she asked her brother, Najid. Her favorite was her mother's cinnamon cake and she hoped that would be the answer.

"I don't know," replied Najid. He was five summers old.

Haniah deflated a little, but her hope returned when she realized there was still the possibility of cinnamon cake.

"I am almost done. If you wait a moment, I'll give it to you to take in to her," said Haniah.

The boy pulled an intricately carved little horse from his pocket that their father had made. The corners of the toy were rounded and the texture of the wood had been smoothed due to frequent use. The boy passed the time by playing with it on his knee. He pretended to make it gallop across a grassy field and then down a multi-colored rainbow, swooping it before his face. His imagination was as boundless as his sister's. And there was much more they had in common. They both loved cinnamon cake, listening to stories told by their mother, and swimming in the pond next to the boulder.

"Did you catch any bish today?" asked Najid, taking a break from his play.

"Bish?" asked Haniah.

"Ya, *bish!*" he said with extra emphasis on the syllable. "You were up at the pond today, weren't you?"

"Oh, fish!" One thing her brother was still working on was pronouncing the sounds of some of his letters. Her parents thought it was cute, to her it was an annoyance. "No, I didn't catch any fish today. I didn't put in a line."

"Did you swim today?"

"No, I didn't swim today."

"What do you do there all the time if you're not bishing or swimming?"

"I think," she said.

"About what?" asked Najid.

She thought for a moment, contemplating what to share with him. "Just stuff." Haniah picked up the bucket and removed the stool. She handed a half-full bucket to her brother who jumped down from the cask. "Take this to Mother."

Holding his wood toy in one hand and the milk in the other, he started back to the house. At the door, he turned to her. "If you do catch a bish next time, be sure to bring it back so we can cook it up."

"Next time I catch a 'bish', I'll be sure to do that." She smiled and turned back to her work. Haniah removed the cow's feed bag and moved over to the pig pen by the time her brother had closed the door behind him.

"And how are you two doing?" she asked. Two large snouts and accompanying eyes looked at her in anticipation of dinner. "Today's menu, provided by your chef, is grass, roots, and corn meal. I do hope you enjoy." She scooped a shovel full of feed and poured it into a trough next to the pen. The pigs stuck their fat heads through the pen's railing and their hungry mouths began to chomp. Haniah placed the shovel back against the wall and leaned over the rough, wood railing. "What a life you both have, being waited on like you are." She leaned back from the pen and ran her hand along the top of the railing.

"Ouch!" Pulling her hand back in pain, she saw a splinter had gotten under her skin. The skin began to turn red where it had gone in. She picked at it with her fingernails, attempting to dislodge it from her palm, but with no success. "First the wolves, the missing stars, the wool, and now this." She let out a groan. They were all under her skin, in a place where she couldn't get to them.

Rubbing her hand along her dress, she tried to forget about the irritation and hoped it, along with the other difficulties, would all go away.

CHAPTER 2

The Map

BY THE TIME HANIAH HAD FINISHED HER CHORES IN THE BARN, THE sun had already fallen behind the tree line, creating a golden glow on the horizon. Darkness would be coming soon. Haniah grabbed a bucket from the barn and headed up a path that led to the well. The path was on a gentle incline and wove through a thicket of trees and brush. The light of day was diminishing and it took several minutes to traverse, but eventually Haniah reached a small clearing where the Well of Aini stood in a circle of worn and faded stones. The stones had been chiseled into square blocks and placed there long before her family had arrived on the farm. Over time, the wind had smoothed them, giving them a polished finish that glistened in the remaining light. The stones sat at knee height, cold and solemn, as if in meditation. Haniah ran her hand across an inscription carved on one of the stones. Whoever had made the markings was long gone.

Haniah placed a knee over the edge of the deep hole and bent over to pull up a bucket of crystal-clear water. Placing the bucket on one of the well's stones, she dipped her hands into the cool water and brought it to her lips. Haniah felt the soothing relief that only these waters could bring; no water was more refreshing than the water drawn from the Well of Aini. After taking another sip of the water, she poured the remainder into the bucket she had brought from the house then turned back to the path home.

As she crossed the farm's clearing, Haniah noticed a light in the barn. The handcart had been moved and she could see her father unloading the wool through the barn's open door. The sheep had all been herded into the pasture behind the barn.

Haniah pushed open the brightly colored door that led into her home. The entire house was filled with the faint smell of cinnamon. A cake was baking in the oven.

She walked into a warm, glowing room lit by oil lamps. One lamp sat on a modest but sturdy oak table in the middle of the room. The others were mounted to thick support beams along the wall. Glass funnels encircled the dancing flames. Haniah had often imagined the flame in the lamps as little yellow and orange fairies caught in a jar.

In one corner sat a finely tailored sitting chair with a spiral fabric pattern. In the other corner sat her mother's wicker rocking chair. When Haniah was younger, she had spent many hours rocking with her mother in that spot.

Between the two chairs was a stone hearth. The fireplace was clean. The weather was warm enough lately that a fire had not been lit for several days. It was a good thing too, as the wood pile next to the house had run low over the winter. Above the fireplace hung the ax used to chop the wood.

At the table, Najid sat on his knees with a book, quietly looking at the pictures drawn in ink. It was a book filled with drawings her father had made of the local wildlife. There was a picture of a badger, a bear, a sparrow, a jay, and a variety of other animals. He turned each page with anticipation. Najid had been through the book a number of times and never seemed to tire of the detailed drawings.

Haniah carried the water into the kitchen where her mother stood cutting vegetables.

"You can set that here." Her mother cleared a place on the counter next to the sink.

Haniah rested the bucket on the counter. "Did Father tell you he didn't sell the wool?"

"He did," said her mother without a pause in her cutting.

"Is this bad?"

"Why would this be bad?" asked her mother, setting the knife to the side and placing a hand on Haniah's shoulder.

"Well, we need supplies to run the farm," said Haniah.

"It's not ideal, but I don't think it's bad," said her mother, turning back to her cutting. "Besides, that's for your father and me to worry about. You have more important things to focus on, like your chores and school work. Speaking of that, have you finished your school work?"

Haniah's mind raced for a response that would not result in her having to do more work. Finally she settled upon the truth. "No."

"Your books are on the table."

Haniah took a seat on the bench next to her brother and opened a book. She picked up the graphite stick sitting next to a piece of paper and began working on the first number problem at the top of the page.

The lamp on the table flickered as her father stepped through the front door. He paused to remove his hat and placed it on a row of crafted hooks next to the door. "I've unloaded all the wool and the sheep have been brought in." He glanced at his kids with a smile, pleased to see them being studious. He walked into the kitchen, poured out some of the water into the plugged sink, and washed his hands with a bar of soap. "That cake smells delicious," he said, taking a deep breath. He bent over to crack open the oven door for a peek.

"You will have to wait until after dinner, Fadi," said her mother playfully to her father. She handed him a towel to dry his hands.

"I just wanted a peek." He took the towel and dried his hands. He set the towel on the counter and walked over to a bookshelf in the living room. Behind a small door, high up on the shelf, he removed a leather binder. He took a seat on the bench across from Haniah and Najid. "How is your book, Najid?" he asked, moving the lamp to one end of the table.

"Good," said Najid. "Did you bring me any sweets brom the village?"

"No, they didn't have any I could buy this time. I am sorry." He reached out and rubbed the boy's moppy hair. Najid smiled and looked back down at his book.

Her father opened the binder, pulled out a piece of parchment, and unfolded it on the table.

"What is that?" asked Haniah.

"A map," said her father. The paper was made of thick, tan paper that had colored over time. The edges were worn. The ink on the page was unlike any she had ever seen. In the light of the lamp it shimmered, as if written with metal.

Haniah stood and walked around the table to lean on her father's shoulder. Looking down, she saw mountains, forests, and lands drawn on the map that she had never heard of. Written on the map she saw the words, *West Kingdom.*

"What's it a map of?" she asked.

"It's a map of the Kingdom of Gathbiyya, also known as the West Kingdom. See, this is where we live." He pointed to a spot on the map that read *Well of Aini.* "And see, there is Stone Bridge."

Najid looked up from his book.

"Are you planning a trip?" asked Haniah.

"I'm not planning on anything for sure, but I want to be prepared," he said.

Mother stopped what she was doing and leaned against the door frame between the kitchen and the living room. She held the towel in her hand, wiping her fingers.

"It's because of what was on the wind today, isn't it?" asked Haniah.

"What gives you that notion?"

"I don't know," she said, looking at the map.

"It may have something to do with the wind. I think I might have to travel a little further to find someone to buy our wool this year."

"Why is that?" asked Haniah.

"Have you ever wondered why the grass grows so green here and the trees so tall, or why there are so many flowers?"

"No, not really. But I am grateful for the flowers."

"It's the well. Some say it's enchanted," said her father.

At those words, a gust of wind blew open the door. It stirred the flames and sent the curtains at the windows into a frenzy. Mother quickly moved to close and lock the door. The wind in the room stopped. Mother straightened her hair away from her face.

"Magic?" asked Haniah with her eyes open wide to her father.

Her mother cleared her throat and moved back to where she stood before. "Not exactly, dear. Your father may be exaggerating a bit too much." She gave him a look.

Fadi looked at Haniah's mother. "Ok." He turned back to Haniah. "It's the well. It kind of acts like a protection for the area." He looked back at his wife, judging her expression. Carefully choosing his words, he continued. "Lately, something has happened to change that."

"Is that why we have wolves?"

"Yes," said her father, hesitating for a moment. "And I may have to go."

"I don't want you to have to go! For how long?"

"Well, I am not even sure if I'll have to. For now, I am just looking at the map."

"Will you go bar?" asked Najid.

"Hopefully not. Maybe just to the next town," said Father.

Haniah had been to Stone Bridge once, but never further. One day's journey was the farthest she had ever been from home. Her father had taken her the season before to trade the wool. The trip was a pleasant experience, just Haniah and her father. They camped outside the village and talked by the campfire the night after they picked up supplies. This year, he said he would make the trip alone as he had before. Haniah did not think anything of it at the time. Now, with this news, it gave her a new perspective on the recent occurrences. Haniah sighed and clenched her fist, then wrinkled her face in pain.

"What is that?" asked her father.

"It's nothing," she said.

"Hold out your hand and let me see."

She placed her hand in front of her body, palm up. Turning on the bench he reached out with calloused fingers and gently held her hand in his. "Looks like you have a nice sliver there. Would you like some help getting it out?"

"I don't know," she said.

"Does it hurt?" he asked.

"Yes."

"Hold still and I'll help." He reached into his pocket with his other hand and pulled out a small, brown pocketknife. He flipped open the short blade.

Haniah pulled her hand away in fear and hid it in the fold of her dress. "No, I don't want that."

"Don't be frightened. This won't hurt any more than the sliver, and it will only hurt for a moment." He kept his hand out and spoke softly. "It's natural to be a little frightened."

Her father had said on occasion that she frightened easily, but that it was expected with her healthy imagination. He always emphasized the healthy part. She was often scared to sleep alone in her own bed. She was frightened of the dark—frightened of what might be lurking under her bed and in her closet. When they lit the fire in the winter time, she had her father keep the fire going until it burned out on its own. The embers glowed, giving a faint light to the cottage that helped ease her fright.

"Haniah is a scaredy cat," taunted Najid.

"Am not!" Heat rose to her face.

"Are too!"

"Well, you don't even know how to pronounce your letters."

"Haniah, please don't argue with your brother," said Mother.

"But he said I'm a scaredy cat." She pointed an accusing finger.

"You're many summers older than your brother. I expect you to act like it."

"That's not fair. Why does he get away with it?" asked Haniah.

"Najid, don't call your sister names," said Fadi, looking at him from across the table.

"It's still not fair," said Haniah.

"Sometimes I wonder if you know just how good you have it here, Haniah," Mother said soothingly. "You're always so helpful. Please help us out now."

"Yes, Mother."

"Give me your hand," said her father.

Timidly, Haniah brought forth her hand and placed it in her father's. One large tear formed in the corner of her eye.

"What is it, Haniah?" asked her father.

"I'm scared." Shaking, she struggled to keep her hand in his.

"It's ok. I haven't even touched you yet." Turning to the table, he shielded her hand from her view. First there was a poke and then a tug. "There, I got it." He let go of her hand. It had ended almost before it had begun. He placed the knife back in his pocket. "See, you got through that trial without any problem."

"I hope I don't have any more trials."

Mother smiled a knowing smile and turned back to the kitchen. "Dinner will be ready soon. Haniah and Najid, can you both please help clear and set the table?"

"Sure, Mother," said Haniah.

Najid climbed down from the bench and placed his book on a shelf.

The wind continued to blow outside. Its howling could now be heard from where the trees surrounded the back of the house. It knocked against the shutters on the windows and the shingles on the roof. For all the turbulence outside, the inside of the home felt cozy and safe. Knowing her father and mother were close made any burden she might have felt seem unimportant. The removal of the sliver had set her at ease and relieved her discomfort. Being with her family was like being curled up next to the fireplace, wrapped in a warm blanket. She breathed easy. She was safe with her family. The trouble with the wolves, the wool, and the stars all felt very far away.

Mother opened the oven and pulled out the cinnamon cake that had been baking for the past hour, setting it on the counter to cool. She lifted the lid on the cast iron pan. The warm edges were perfectly golden and the sweet smell permeated the air. Haniah breathed deeply as she helped set the table. Her mother was right, sometimes Haniah didn't realize how good of a life she had. Between the chores, school work, and play time, there was love and security. And there was nothing that was going to change that.

CHAPTER 3

The Traveler

HANIAH STOPPED WHERE SHE STOOD, HOLDING HER BOOKS IN HER hands. She frowned at the door, certain she had imagined the knock. Her father froze with the map folded under his arm. Both Haniah's mother and brother looked to her father.

It could have been the wind. No one except her family traveled the unmarked Southern Path and Haniah could not remember the last visitor they received. No one spoke. No one moved. The whistling of the wind passed over the house.

Again came the knock, thist time more direct and more distinct. It wasn't the wind. Someone was at the door.

Haniah's father stood and walked to the door. His hand hovered only for a second before he unlocked the latch then twisted the handle open. A whirlwind of a shape seemed to pour inside. A woman straightened before them, one hand holding onto her pointed hat as her cape swirled about her in the wind. She moved in through the doorway and past Haniah's father as if the wind dictated her moves. The door was quickly closed and the room became still once again. "Very fine wind storm this evening," spoke the woman as she placed the tip of her staff upon the wooden floorboards. "Thank you so kindly for opening up." She smoothed down her skirt as she addressed Haniah's father who still stood by the door.

"Who has graced this residence with her company this evening, and how shall she be addressed?" asked her father as politely as his surprise would allow.

"I am but a beggar, an old woman, lowly and humble in my supplications. You may call me Madam Nuwairah," said the woman. She entered further into the room and looked over the table and lighting.

"What brings you out on a night like tonight, and here in our hills?" asked Haniah's father.

"I am a poor wanderer. I seek knowledge I have not yet obtained." The woman continued her inspection of her surroundings as she answered. She walked past Haniah's father and over to the bookshelf. She placed her nose an inch from the book bindings as if inspecting each one for dust or, perhaps, smelling them.

Haniah's father shrugged his shoulders to his wife and then turned his attention back to the woman. Najid moved out of the woman's way as she passed by him, the chairs, and the fireplace. She ran her finger along the top of a closed chest and peered out the window into the dark. She touched the colored fabric that hung in the window. "Very charming cottage you have," she said, speaking to no one in particular. Circling the room, she came back to stand in front of Haniah's father. She squinted as her gaze tracked from the bottom of his feet up to the top of his head. "Who, may I ask, might you be, and whereupon have I found myself?"

Haniah's father hesitated for a moment, then seemed to determine that the woman was not a specter come to torment his family. "My name is Fadi. This is Kamilah, my wife." He gestured to her mother who stood by the kitchen. "You're in our home, located in the West Hills of Aini. I am a farmer and tender of the land."

The woman pointed her finger toward Kamilah as if to say something, but soon became lost in her own thoughts. She turned back to Haniah's father, Fadi, and stared at him with a blank face. She teetered there for a moment on her heels with her finger extended.

"Would you like to come in and have a seat? We were just about to put dinner on. Would you like to join us?" asked Fadi, gently holding the woman's elbow.

The woman balanced herself and cocked her head to one side. "I would greatly appreciate it. I am famished." Lowering her finger she looked at the staff in her other arm but not at anyone else in the room. "It has been a long day, and I have not made time to take supper."

"Can I take your cape and staff?" Fadi asked as he moved to help her with her cape.

"No, that will not be necessary. I prefer to keep them both at my side," said the stranger.

"Please, have a seat here." He helped her into the rocking chair. "Could I interest you in some tea?"

"Yes, please." The stranger leaned her polished wood staff against the chair.

Turning away from the woman, Fadi set the map on the bookshelf and spoke. "Kids, help your mother set the table. I'll get our guest some tea."

Haniah moved into the kitchen and took the bowls from her mother who had them waiting for her on the counter. Najid took the spoons from his mother and followed his big sister back into the front room where they began to place the items around the table.

After a moment, her father carried in a tray with a teapot and cups. He set it on a table next to the woman and poured a cup of tea. The woman took the cup from her host. "This is a most interesting little cup. What do you call this?" She held the cup to her face and pointed to the handle.

"Umm…" Fadi stammered. "That's a handle. You hold it with your fingers."

"How charming." The woman giggled. "I don't recall ever seeing such a splendid little cup in all my travels." Holding the handle by the tips of her fingers, she took a sip. "Yes, charming!" The more Haniah watched the woman, the more it became apparent that she was not ordinary. The woman had a hard time balancing both her body and her thoughts.

"Where are you from?" asked Fadi.

"I don't quite recall," the woman replied between her sips of tea.

"You don't know where you're from?" asked Haniah's mother with a puzzled look.

"That is true, but of little concern," said the old woman. "I do remember, however, why I am about and the errand I am upon. It is a matter I wish to discuss with your husband, once I am done enjoying my tea."

Najid placed wood cups at each table setting and Haniah came behind, filling them with a water pitcher. Kamilah carried a large pot of stew and placed it on the table. "Dinner is ready," she said. "Children, wash your hands."

They washed their hands as their father helped the old woman out of her chair and over to the table.

"Najid, will you help get our guest's chair for her?" asked his father. Najid pulled out the chair next to the woman. The stranger startled as she looked down at the little boy who had just moved her chair. She looked up and was surprised to see Haniah seating herself at the table.

"Where did they come from?" asked the woman, waving a hand at Haniah and Najid. Evidently, she had not noticed the children in the room until now.

The more Haniah saw of this woman, the less threatening she became to her family and the more threatening she became to herself. Haniah pictured the unaware woman lost, wandering about the land and walking off a cliff.

"I wonder if she has hit her head?" she whispered to her mother next to her.

Kamilah patted Haniah on the leg as if to tell her to be kind.

The old woman sat in a chair at the head of the table. Haniah sat on the bench next to her. With everyone sitting, Fadi placed his hands together and bowed his head. His wife and children did the same. "Our dear Creator. We thank you for this meal. We thank you for our guest and her safe travels. Bless our home." Haniah peeked and saw that the woman did not fold her hands or bow her head. Fadi ended his prayer and invited all to help themselves to the meal.

Kamilah poured the rabbit stew into the children's bowls. Haniah took a sip with pleasure. Her mother blew on Najid's hot stew before he would try his.

The woman stared blankly into her empty bowl and, in a distant voice, began to talk.

The hearts of men fail them and the stars refuse to shine.
Then shall the darkness come.

She looked up from her bowl at Fadi, sitting at the other end of the table. "That is the prophecy. There is a rumor of darkness spreading across the land. Some have said they have seen dark armies forming on the borders of the kingdom."

Kamilah stiffened and slowly laid down her spoon.

"What is this you speak of?" asked Fadi, leaning forward over the table.

"Even here you must have noticed that the stars have faded and the moon no longer reflects its glow upon the land. People are becoming cruel and callous," the woman said in a shallow voice.

"We have noticed," he said. "What do you think it means, and what word do you bring from your travels?"

"Fadi," said Kamilah in a tone that indicated she would rather this subject not be talked about.

"It's ok, dear." He placed a gentle hand on her arm.

"Centuries ago, the three kingdoms allied to keep out the darkness of the world." The traveling woman spoke even softer.

Haniah leaned in to hear.

"Magical gifts were bestowed upon the West Kingdom and were placed around the kingdom as protectors. These enchanted relics were granted the ability to keep evil forces from entering the kingdom." The woman looked far into the distance, as if knowing she was weaving a tale sure to intrigue the children.

"What kind of relics?" asked Haniah.

"Gems!" exclaimed the woman. The word passed from her mouth with a burst of feeling and a gesture from her outstretched hands. "They were given to the king's ancestors many generations ago. It was three hundred summers since the last darkening, before the new light was brought into the world. The four Gems of Anwar were taken and hidden at that time around the borders of the kingdom. There they have stayed these many summers and for these many summers the kingdom has lived in peace and light." The woman paused to let what she was saying sink in.

Both children sat wide-eyed, their mouths open.

"Close your mouths children. We are not cattle," scolded their mother, then turned her gaze upon the stranger. "Surely Madam Nuwairah, this is all lore and speculation. You cannot expect us to believe such things."

"The enchantments are weakening. You must admit that you see the effects even here in the West Hills."

"We have wolves!" Haniah interjected with enthusiasm.

The woman nodded but said not a word, letting Haniah's statement punctuate her argument.

Mother did not respond.

"What is the business of the evening you're upon and the errand you alluded to earlier?" asked Fadi.

"I am on an errand to find the king," said Madam Nuwairah. "The rightful ruler of Gathbiyya. He will bring forth the Golden Gem, restore the light, and save us from the darkness that threatens to destroy this kingdom."

He looked into the faces of his children. "I am sure the king will be along as soon as he can," said her father. "Though I be just a farmer here, I am confident of this—I believe the king would not desert his stewardship. He will not leave his kingdom nor its people to perish."

With her father's words, a look of awareness came to the woman's eyes that had not been there before. She looked into the faces of those sitting around the table, and the flame of the lamp twinkled in her eye.

"Please, I would ask that we stop speaking of this topic," said Mother. "It is liable to frighten the children. They don't need more to entice their imaginations."

"Yes, we will change the subject," agreed Father. "Thank you for the news you have brought, Madam Nuwairah." He gave a cordial nod. Something in the unspoken gesture passed between her father and the stranger, but Haniah couldn't quite make it out.

"Please pass the stew," said the woman, holding up her bowl. Fadi filled her bowl and she began to eat. "Thank you for allowing me to eat with you. Your kindness and generosity will be rewarded. If not by me, then by the Creator."

The woman was peculiar. She was short and wore an outfit of bluish grey. At first glance it appeared to be a beggar's garb with a patch here and a patch there, but upon further observation it was clear the outfit was nothing of the sort. The wool was finely spun and the stitching on the hem was expertly done. A thin insignia of gold ran along the hem of her tunic, small enough not to notice unless one was sitting right next to her.

True care had gone into the creation of the clothing. Haniah could not say she had ever seen finer made clothing than what the stranger sitting next to her wore.

They continued their meal in silence. Haniah glanced at the woman with each bite she took.

Having finished her bowl of stew, Madam Nuwairah grasped her staff in hand and stood. "I must be going," she said abruptly. "I have much to do and many more leagues to travel before my night is through."

"Stay for cake, will you?" asked Haniah, hoping the woman might share more than she already had.

"I cannot, child. I must be about my errand." She spoke the words kindly. Then she turned to Haniah's mother. "Upon my leaving, may I have a moment of privacy with your husband, outside maybe?"

Kamilah looked to her husband, weighing the question in her mind. A longing drifted through her gaze. "Yes," she said, still intent upon her husband. Fadi reached out and held the hand she had placed on the table next to him. He held it there for a moment and let go. He stood and moved toward the door.

Only when the door was opened to show the old woman out did Haniah notice that it was quiet outside. The wind had stopped as quickly as it had come. It had left as if it had been there only to carry a message and leave. They closed the door behind them and left Haniah, her brother, and her mother alone in the room.

"Let's clear the table, children," said her mother. She made a little pile with the bowls and handed them to Haniah. The spoons she gave to Najid. Her hands shook as she picked up the pot the stew had been in. She tightened her grip on the handles.

"Are you ok, Mother?" asked Haniah.

"Yes, dear."

"What do you think they are talking about?" asked Haniah.

"I do not want to imagine what is being spoken," said her mother solemnly as she placed the pot in the sink.

Najid ran over to the window to peer out into the darkness.

"Come away from there, Najid. Let them have their privacy." Kamilah motioned with her arm for her child to come to her. She pulled Haniah next to her side and reached out to hold Najid's hand as he came over.

There she stood, holding them when the door opened. With a long and direct stride, Fadi came back in the home.

"Lock the shutters on all the windows." He spoke with haste. "Close the grate on the fireplace and lock the door behind me. I'll be back in a moment."

"What is it, dear?" asked her mother.

"It is what we have feared." He grabbed the axe hanging above the fireplace. "Haniah, come with me." Not waiting for a response, he turned to leave. Haniah stood still for a moment, looking at her mother. Her motherther gestured for her to follow her father. Together, father and daughter walked out of the house and into the darkness.

CHAPTER 4

Attacked at Night

FEAR PIERCED HANIAH'S HEART LIKE THE HARSH PAIN OF A HORNET'S sting. She no longer felt the comfort of her home as she followed her father across the clearing and past the barn. He took urgent steps and Haniah ran to keep up. The light diminished as they moved from what little light the farm windows offered and onto the trail to the well. She followed the sound of the shadow in front of her. What danger would require her father to carry an axe? Surely wolves would not come this close to the house. She pictured in her mind the vicious teeth and yellow eyes of wolves prowling the land. The fear settled into a knot in the bottom of her stomach. Noticing she was falling a step behind, she quickened her pace and almost ran into the back of her father.

For Haniah, the trail was indiscernible, the footing treacherous, but her father was able to see in the dark with his keen sense of sight and he led the way. In her haste, she stumbled on rocks and roots. Haniah looked up into the dark sky. "That woman who came tonight, does she know where the stars have gone?"

"I do not know," said Father. "The stars are our ancestors, Haniah. They are your grandparents and their grandparents. All those who have come before us. When they leave this world they do not die, but move to the heavens." Her father didn't break his pace.

"Yes, I know that, but will they come back?" asked Haniah.

"I have hope that they will. The stars stand as our guides. They provide light in the darkness. Sailing captains have used the stars to guide their ships over stormy seas. Explorers have used them to traverse rugged terrain and to see the world. They give us hope. Without them, all people would be lost and the world would not progress as it does." They entered the clearing around the well and approached the waiting structure. Her father sat on one of its square stones and peered down into the bleak hole below. In the darkness, Haniah could only make out the dark outline of her father. "Yes, I have hope. But the fact remains that the stars have faded, and if they fade for too long, I fear they are in danger of not returning."

Haniah felt a lump form in the back of her throat. To imagine the world in this kind of darkness for any prolonged amount of time caused the fear sitting heavy in her stomach to roll.

"The fading of the stars is only the beginning of the true threat. It is a sign that the hearts of men are beginning to fail." Her father leaned over into the well. He reached down with his hand and removed a stone that had been lodged in the well's wall.

"What does that mean?"

"It means a dark shadow is falling over the world. The people of the world are changing." He stuck his hand in the crevice the stone had filled and brought out the end of a rope. "Your mother would not like me sharing these stories with you, but I think it is important for you to know. The hearts of men are becoming callous, unkind, and greedy. It is an evil our family has not had to endure until this time. I do believe we will have to be strong." He pulled on the rope, one hand over the other until a satchel appeared tied to the end of the rope. It was made of leather and had a strap so that it could be worn. Fadi freed the satchel from the rope and held it up in his hands.

The markings that had been carved on the well began to give a faint glow, just a trickle. So little light flowed that she would not have noticed it if her eyes had not adjusted to the dark. The markings changed their shapes into a script. "What is that?" asked Haniah as she looked at the markings and took a step closer to her father. A dim blue haze fell upon the ground around them.

"That is writing," said her father. "I wanted you to see this."

"Can you read it?" she asked.

"Here, that which is hidden will be kept safe. To the guardian is given power and might," he read.

"What does it—?" Fadi raised his hand to keep Haniah from finishing her thought. He tilted his ear and listened to the darkness. In the brush, a stick snapped. Haniah could feel her heart pound. Something was in the woods.

"Get to the house. Fast." He held her arm and spoke in a hushed and stern tone. "Now, run!" With her arm released, she ran for the trail. A shadow jumped from the trees behind the well and let out a growl that sounded like death itself. Fadi turned and ran. "Hurry, Haniah!" he called behind her.

Her feet raced over the uneven ground. Branches whipped her arms and legs as she ran blindly into the night. More noises came from the woods—grunts and snarls that chilled the spine. They could be heard from the distance behind and to the sides of her. She stumbled and fell, the palms of her hands sliding on gravel. She could hear branches breaking and growls growing closer quickly. Just as they were upon her, a firm hand lifted her up from behind and placed her on her feet.

"Run, Haniah!" begged her father. She ran harder than she had ever run before, down the hill, across the clearing and to the cottage door. "Open up!" she screamed, banging on the door. The door opened and she fell in through the doorway. She struggled to catch her breath. Father quickly followed and slammed the door shut, locking the bolt behind him.

He moved to the table in the room. Lifting it up on one end, he threw it against the door, jamming it in place with his foot. "Everyone keep away from the windows," he said, looking around the room. He held the ax at his side and the satchel over his shoulder.

"What is it, Father?" panted Haniah.

"Goblins!"

"What? Here?" Her mother picked up Najid and held him tightly in her arms.

"But that can't be. Goblins are only in stories!" Haniah protested.

A thundering boom hit against the front of the house and was accompanied by some terrifying growls. The door bowed and the table shook. Haniah tensed as a picture fell to the floor.

"They will be looking for a way in," said Fadi, moving to the bookshelf where he had placed the map. He picked up the map, stuffed it in the satchel, and drew up the tie to close it. "Hold this," he said, moving to Haniah. "Whatever you do, don't let go of this." He held out the satchel for her to take.

She took the satchel from her father with both hands. Immediately she felt a warm, tingling sensation. It began at the tips of her fingers, then moved to her hands. The warmth migrated along her arms and into her chest where it nearly burst from within. The feeling continued moving through her entire body down to her toes and up to the crown of her head. So complete was the covering of her entire frame with this feeling that she would have thought she had just slipped into a warm bath. Surprisingly, the knot of fear loosened slightly, allowing her a moment to think. The faint smell from the cake baking suddenly filled her nostrils, and she could pick out the individual spices. The colors on the curtains became more vibrant, popping when she looked at them. Everything seemed to be peaceful for just one moment.

A large crash from outside brought Haniah back to her situation. This time, little pieces of ceiling fell to the floor.

Her family huddled together, not knowing which direction to turn. All around them the sounds echoed in the room like a large drum being pounded. The booming continued as the scraping and banging moved along the walls and onto the roof. The rafters shook. Haniah looked to the ceiling where she could hear feet and claws moving. "They are by the chimney," Haniah said, moving away from the fireplace and placing her back up against a wall.

A large fist crashed through the shutters next to Haniah. Frantically, Haniah struggled to get away from the blistered black hands that grabbed at her. Gnarled flesh crowded the opening and threatened to pull her through the broken glass. Frantic claws left scars in the broken wood frame and on the shutters. Without hesitation, Fadi was at his daughter's side fighting to free her from flailing appendages. He pushed her aside and moved them both to the center of the room.

What broke through the shutters next was worse than any wolf Haniah had ever seen. The twisted face that presented itself was beyond hideous and more terrifying than any evil she could have imagined. Red, bloody eyes peered through the melee. A sinister grin lined with razor teeth twisted and foamed as it growled with a spasm.

More breaking glass and crashing came from the other windows around the room. The cacophony of broken wood and snarling razor teeth mingled with Najid's cries. He clung to his mother, frantic to get away from the nightmares attacking his home.

There were too many for Fadi to focus on. He spun around, waiting for the walls to fall and the first lunge to come.

Several bloated figures crashed through the windows. The muscular and smelly creatures clamored and scraped at each other to be the first to get at the family. They leapt first for Fadi.

The first one met Fadi's axe and fell to the floor, but the second threw itself into Fadi. They fell against the other side of the room. The two struggled as a third and fourth goblin overtook him in a pile of biting and snarling.

The door to the cottage blew off its hinges, sending the table crashing to the floor. The lamps in the room blew out. Darkness engulfed the family. A sinister cheer roared from the clamorous crowd of goblins still outside. Filling the doorway stood Evil in human form. He wore a velvet robe, dark as midnight with crimson trim on the hood and sleeves. He held a tall, charcoal staff in his hand, topped with a red gem that began to pulse with a glow, illuminating the room in wine-colored shadows.

In the red light, Haniah could now see her father, restrained under a pile of monsters. Powerful hands held his head to the ground, his cheek to the floor. His brow grimaced in pain. Her mother stood fearfully huddled in the corner with Najid.

The figure in the doorway enchanted a spell with his lips. He set his attention upon her father and the pile of goblins tousling on the floor. Fadi's skin began to glow red, the glow grew brighter and brighter, then her father was gone. Haniah tried to blink away the bright image of her father burned into her vision after the light was extinguished. Her mother began to sob. She cowered into the corner, trying to shield her son from their doom. Haniah took a step toward the kitchen, slowly backing away from the menacing figure. The black-robed man's attention was upon Kamilah when he began his chant again. Both Kamilah and her son began to glow red like her husband had, until the light lit the entire room. Then they vanished. The room was once again left in the cold, red glow of the gem on the staff.

Haniah was alone. She gripped the satchel to her chest.

Evil turned his attention to her. "There it is. I can feel it," said a cold, vile voice from beneath its hood. "Hand me the bag."

Her breath caught as time stopped. The red pulse of the light stilled, and her heart gave no pulse. All that stood before her was fear. All that existed was terror. She could not move. The darkness of the figure sucked her in as if to consume her soul. Frozen in place and unable to do anything, she shrank in fear.

Behind Haniah the kitchen door from the back of the cottage was flung wide with a gust of wind that shook the house and all those in it. A blinding white light followed.

The dark figure raised his arm to shield his eyes.

"Get behind me," said a voice from the white light. A woman's cape and hair streamed in the wind. With outstretched arms, she slammed the point of her staff on the kitchen floor. Haniah stood stiff, unable to process all that was happening. The woman grabbed Haniah by the arm and pushed her through the kitchen and out the back door. "Run, girl, run!"

Haniah ran to the back porch. She did not stay to see the woman turn back into the house. She ran with no direction in mind. She just ran! There was an explosion and then the cottage erupted into flames. The blast knocked Haniah to the ground. She looked back to see haunting figures framed in a gold and yellow wash of firelight. She could see the flickers of twenty pairs of eyes in pursuit, wielding clubs and swords. She lifted herself up off the ground and ran, weaving through the trees.

The night was dark, but the burning of the farm lit the trees' trunks. Long, stark shadows were cast across the forest. Haniah could hear the snarling and grunting coming ever closer. She ducked behind a tree as two of the horrid creatures passed by. She waited, counting to ten, thent she ran again, changing her direction. A call from one of the creatures sounded. They had seen her flee from her hiding spot.

A burly, blistered body pounced from behind a rock. Its crushing weight landed on her as they fell to the ground. Haniah cried out as she hit her head.

Out of the darkness came a person wielding a shining sword. The grip of the sword landed squarely upon the head of the goblin that had pulled her to the ground. Haniah lifted herself to one knee in an attempt to stand. Her vision turned foggy, her balance unstable.

Next to her, the figure with the sword jumped and kicked as one goblin after another lunged to attack then fell to the ground. Haniah could make out the movements of the sword as it glistened and flickered with the light of her burning home. It was too dark to make out anything else but the shadows. The shadows became darker as Haniah faded out of consciousness.

CHAPTER 5

Cinnamon Cake

THE MORNING SUN CREPT UP FROM THE WEST, STREAKING GOLD beams of light through a grove of trees on the western hills. They decorated the woodland like drapes of transparent silk. A peaceful dew glistened on the foliage, making the area appear as though it had been touched by an angelic spirit. In the distance, a bird welcomed the day with a sweet harmonic song that swooped in pitch once and was gone. The previous night's events had been subdued and a soothing aura hung in the air.

Haniah lay on the ground, she gave a soft moan as she raised her head. A woman moved from where she was perched, sitting on a log. "There, child. Don't move too quickly. You have been through a lot."

Foggy images and visions came to the Haniah's mind. Cloudy memories of bloody teeth mixed with fear and darkness, a flash of light. A dull pain throbbed in her head. She raised a hand to her forehead.

"You took quite a bump to your head," said the woman. "I have done what I can to ease the pain."

Pain. "*Pain,*" moaned Haniah. She experienced a sudden awareness of the rest of her body. Her body felt sore. She could feel pain on the palms of her hands as she placed them in front of her face. They were scraped and bloodied from where she had fallen on the trail, running from the noises in the night. In all the excitement, she had not noticed them until now.

"They will need tending to," said the woman gently. "I did not want to wake you."

Haniah looked around at the trees and brush. In the distance, through the towering woods, she could see a plume of smoldering smoke still lingering above the remains of her home. A charred ruin of wood and stone lay in the clearing. A solemn hush washed over the area. "How long have I been out?" she asked.

"Not long. A few hours." The woman took a cloth rag from the folds of her skirt. Holding the cloth in her hands, the woman whispered an incantation, turning the rag cold. The cool rag was placed on Haniah's head. "This will help you feel better," she said.

"What happened?" asked Haniah. There were many gaps in her memory from the night before.

"Evil has arrived and the world is no longer safe."

"I saw you last night," said Haniah. "You came to dinner. Then you came back to us. You had a light. Who are you?"

"I am the wizardess Nuwairah," said the woman. "The First Wizardess of the Three Circles." She held out her hands with a small bar of soap. Haniah grimaced from the sting as her hands were washed and rinsed with water emptied from a metal canteen. "The water came from the well. My magic and its healing properties should have you mended in no time." They both watched as the wounds began to close and scabbing began to form.

"Thank you," said Haniah, looking around once again. "Where is the hero? I have to thank him too."

"What hero?" asked the wizardess.

"The one from last night," she said with a new energy in her voice. "The one who saved me. The one with the sword."

"That hero," said Nuwairah with understanding in her comment. "That hero has gone."

She looked over the woman's shoulder, but no one else was there. The girl sunk back down into the grass, no longer hopeful about meeting a real hero. With that small loss, the weight of what happened began to creep into her spirit. "My family," she said.

"There are four of them." said Nuwairah redirecting the girl's attention.

Haniah looked up at the woman. "Four of what?"

"Four gems," said the woman. "They are protective emblems placed around the kingdom three hundred summers ago to protect the land and its people. They were placed in fortresses, secret places and hard to get to places. The darkness comes in search of them and their power. With them, the evil intends to destroy the world."

Haniah felt a sinking in her soul.

"There is prophecy about a Golden Gem that will save the world," said Nuwairah who began to recite the words:

"And in that day the darkness will win.
The Golden Gem will be revealed, its magic shall conquer all."

"This isn't true. Magic is only in stories and books," Haniah protested.

"What is it you think you saw last night?" asked the wizardess.

Haniah remembered her father, her mother, and brother all disappearing in a red glow. She could remember a white light and wind, a blast that threw her to the ground. She did not speak.

"I assure you, it is not only in books," said the First Wizardess of the Three Circles.

She could see Haniah was still processing this information from the look of concentration on the girl's face. She continued, "Those who look for the gems are called seekers. The seeker who finds a stone can wield power to either save or to destroy. But to protect this great power, a gem is protected by a guardian." The woman paused for Haniah's benefit. "Are you following?"

"Yes, I believe so. There are guardians to protect the gems."

"Correct," said Nuwairah. "They protect them from seekers, ones who would wish to possess the gems. Only a true seeker for good can become a guardian."

"What is a true seeker?" asked Haniah, sitting up with interest.

"Someone of pure heart." The woman walked over to where she had been sitting and picked up the leather bag her father had given her. "How did you come by this satchel?" she asked, holding the bag up to Haniah.

"My father gave it to me."

"Then you are a guardian."

"What do you mean, 'I am a guardian?'" Haniah asked emphatically.

"Within this bag is a gem." The woman looked at Haniah with eyes that pressed for an answer. "Your father was a guardian. If he gave this bag to you, then you are now the guardian."

"I am not a guardian!" Haniah spoke quickly. "How can my father be a guardian?" She was bewildered as she grasped for an answer. Confusion ran like a wild horse through her thoughts.

"He was entrusted with the gem from another guardian," said Nuwairah.

"Why did he never say anything about this?"

"I am not the one to tell you these things. Your father will have to tell you more when you have saved him."

"Saved him? Do you mean he is not dead?" asked Haniah, a speck of optimism in her voice. Her big, brown eyes focused hard on the woman.

"I do not believe so." She glanced up into the sky for a moment as if looking for something unseen. "No, they are not dead. Rather, they are captured." A few fluffy white clouds blew overhead as she turned back to the girl who listened with eager ears. "If they had died, they would have gone the way of the unknown and there would not be an essence of their existence within our view." She held up the satchel in her hand. "You must seek out the remaining three gems. Only then will the Golden Gem of Anwar be revealed and only then can your family be saved. But you must act fast. The longer it takes to find the gems the further away and more entrapped your family will become. And the task to save them is already difficult enough."

Hearing her family was alive brought a spark of hope, but the hope was fading fast as the woman continued. "If taken too long, they will not be savable and will be lost forever. Then it can be said they are dead." The words squelched her hope.

"Can't the gem we have here bring them back? You just said they could be saved. Can't we go now and save them?" asked Haniah.

"Save them from captivity?" asked Nuwairah. "No. The power they were taken with is too strong for the magic of this one gem alone. But with all four gems their chances of rescue increase."

"If we don't get to them in time," asked Haniah, "then can the gems save them from death?"

"The gems do not have the power to bring the dead back to life," responded the wizardess. "The gem gives strength to the powers a guardian already possesses. It heightens their abilities. It cannot give new abilities to the guardian if he or she does not already possess the desired skills. So no, it cannot bring people back to life. You must save them before they die."

Haniah's eyes lowered as her shoulders slumped. Inside, she could feel every hope she had ever had being crumbled. Her world was being taken away and in return she was being given nothing. Nothing substantial she could put her faith in. She had a woman who, just the night before, was clueless to her surroundings and now spoke of magic and rocks. Rocks that could not grant to her any special power to provide any hope of finding her family. A deep darkness washed over her mind.

"Look at it in a new light and do not get discouraged," said Nuwairah. "As it is, they are not dead. They are entrapped. I used my magic last night to keep them alive. We are not helpless. We have a say in this as we do in all things." The wizardess stood tall, holding her staff at her side. "You must go and seek out the remaining gems before it is too late. You must reveal the Golden Gem before the evil from last night finds it and uses it for its evil purposes."

"I can't do that," Haniah said, not moving from where she sat. "I have no powers, no talents the gems can strengthen." She did not look up. "What about the hero from last night? Why can't he do it?"

Kneeling down on the ground, the woman lifted Haniah's chin. Nuwairah's face softened as she looked Haniah in the eye. "There are powerful friends who fight the darkness and to each they are given their own tasks. The hero of last night is on an errand." Taking the girl's arm, she gently helped Haniah to her feet. "You must be like the hero you saw last night. You have been charged with your own task to guard the gem your father gave you. Seek out the remaining gems and save your family."

"I can't do all that," said Haniah with earnest. "I am afraid." She lowered her head again.

Nuwairah helped Haniah to a fallen tree where they both sat. "There is something I wish to give you to help you with your fear," spoke Nuwairah as she brought forth a clasped hand from a fold in her skirt. The woman unfurled her fingers. In the palm of her hand sat a polished silver charm attached to a chain. The woman took Haniah's hand and placed the necklace in it.

Haniah lifted it up by its chain. It spun and glistened in the early morning light. The craftsmanship was meticulous. Detailed images of what looked like flowers and birds decorated its surface. She had never seen such a beautiful piece of jewelry.

"It opens," said Nuwairah, pointing to a small clasp on its side.

Haniah opened it to reveal a flat surface of blue glass. It gave a faint glow. In the glass was an image of the old woman sitting in front of her, as clear as looking at the actual person. Then, the picture moved. Haniah's eyes widened. For the second time in less than a day, she was seeing magic. The woman smiled, both in real life and in the pocket sized silver piece. "What is this?" asked Haniah.

"It is a director," said the wizardess. "It is a compass that points to the pure in heart." The woman pointed a finger to the border of the glass. A small green arrow pointed in the direction of the woman pointing.

Haniah moved the locket from side to side and watched as the arrow followed the woman. "This is amazing," said Haniah.

"It is by this director that I was able to find your farm," said Nuwairah. "You are to take it and travel to Stone Bridge. There you will find someone who can help you. This will ensure you find someone with a pure heart."

Haniah closed the magic item. She could not guess how such a device detected what was in someone's heart, let alone find the person. "If you found the farm by using this magic necklace, how did they find my family?" asked Haniah.

"Who?" questioned Nuwairah.

"The goblins."

"I believe they have a witheram."

"What's a witheram?"

"A twisted creature with the ability to smell magic. Only the darkest of evil spawn have the ability to track the scent of magic. The magic of the gem would have led it here," said Nuwairah.

"Wait," replied Haniah in alarm. "You say this thing can smell the scent of a gem, and you want me to keep it?"

"Precisely," said the woman matter-of-factly. "Once a goblin, but twisted by dark magic, a witheram seeks out magic relics and those who can wield them. They have filed teeth, vein-covered skin and bloodshot eyes."

"You have got to be kidding me!"

"I tell you this so you know what to look out for." Nuwairah stood and lifted Haniah up by the arm. "You must be moving. The goblins will be back in the night to seek out what they did not find the night before. They know the gem is here. Best that it be as far from here as possible when they return."

Haniah held out her hand to give the silver necklace back.

"You keep it. It is yours."

"Thank you." Haniah timidly placed the necklace around her neck. "Why don't you take it?" asked Haniah.

"Take the necklace?"

"Take the Gem."

"I can't," said the wizardess. "It is to you that it has been given. You are now the guardian. I have other things I must tend to before the end comes."

"What do you mean 'before the end comes'?" questioned Haniah.

"Before the darkness overruns the world as spoken of in the prophecies," she said, lowering her voice as she leaned into Haniah. "It is safest to travel in the day. Goblins like the dark and will be out at night." Haniah gave a shiver that travelled from the back of her neck and down to the tip of her fingers.

To change the subject, the woman held the satchel up and untied the top. Reaching into the bag she pulled out a metal flask with a screwed top. Holding it firmly, she spoke a few words in a tongue Haniah could not understand. The flask and its contents chilled. "That will keep it cool." She placed the flask back in the bag and looked inside. "I believe one of your favorites has been placed in here for you to eat," she said, looking up at Haniah. "I am instructed to tell you that when you do stop to eat and drink, you are to drink deeply. I am told it will give you strength for your journey ahead."

"Who told you that?" asked Haniah.

"There isn't time to talk further." She closed the satchel and handed it to Haniah. "You must be on your way." The woman embraced her in a hug and whispered in her ear, "Be brave."

The wizardess let go of her embrace, turned Haniah to the south, and gently pushed Haniah's back with her hand as she began to walk. Haniah glanced behind to see the wizardess watching her walk away.

⚜⚜

Haniah walked in a daze with no true ambition, like a twig carried by the currents of a stream. Her task, she knew, was daunting, but she thought of her family being lost forever and her feet continued forward. Being untraveled in the world and of relatively few summers, she knew her chances of success were slim. Yet, she walked. She put one foot in front of the other, with no notion of how many steps she would ultimately need to take. She did not think far ahead, for if she did, she would have cowered in despair. For despair truly lingered wherever she looked. Despair traveled the Southern Path she took with her feet and the inward path she took with her soul. But still she walked.

She traveled the Southern Path that morning alone. She did not think many thoughts along that path. She did not have the luxury. Any unprotected thought had the possibility of hindering her progress. If she thought upon the horrors she had witnessed the past day, she was likely to stop cold in fear. If she thought upon her missing family, she was likely to stop in grief.

Early morning turned to midmorning, and then noon. After an uncounted number of steps, she thought about how nice it would be to have a horse. The farm did not have any horses, on account of their cost. Her family had enough money to get by each season, but nothing was spent on something that was not needed. A horse was a want on the family farm. Not a need. Family farm. Her family. What she wouldn't give to be with them now.

It had been a half hour since she turned off the Southern Path and onto the Gold Road. The road was made of white, packed dirt with shallow ruts. It was wide enough for two wagons to pass to either side and was more trafficked than the path she had come from. Still she had not passed nor seen anyone. She had been hungry for an hour before thoughts of stopping for rest became an interest. Her feet were beginning to get sore.

She crossed the road to a large whisper oak tree that sat off the road among leafy brush. Removing her pack, she leaned her back against the smooth trunk of the tree and stretched out her feet in front of her.

She looked up into the sky. Above the tree, the sun had reached its peak directly overhead and was on its way back down. If she hurried, she would make it to Stone Bridge before nightfall. Before danger. There she imagined the people of the town she had visited once before with her father.

They were good country people. Her father had sold their wool to a tall, lean man who was friendly to her father. There she had bought a book from the merchant peddler about an orphan who lived in a kingdom and had traded places with a prince. It was a delightful tale she thought of fondly. Haniah knew she would find people to help her. Perhaps they would gather a search party to find her family. Together the town would save them. All would be well once she arrived at the village. It was with these encouraging thoughts that she opened her bag.

Reaching in with two hands, she brought out a radiant, white gem and held it up to her eyes. Its smooth edges reflected the light into a million tiny rainbows. She cupped the gem, balancing its weight between her two hands. Its substantial size would have made the richest king jealous. Haniah had no way to fathom its worth. She slowly turned it from side to side just to see the light radiate out. Like so many of her experiences the past few days, she had never seen anything like it.

She carefully placed the gem back into its bag, then reverently retrieved a little wooden toy horse, carved from a single piece of wood she had seen her father working on. She remembered her brother, Najid, playing with it while sitting on a cask in their barn. She remembered his scruffy hair and his thin little arms. Her heart swelled within her as she imagined how much she would love to see him once again. She placed the toy lovingly next to her.

Reaching into the satchel once again, she retrieved a wooden bowl that had a lid tied to the top and the flask the wizardess had cooled with a spell. Setting the flask next to her other side, she untied the bowl on her lap. Inside was a piece of her mother's cinnamon cake. She smiled at the memory of her mother baking the cake the night before. She thought of her mother's apron and the way she was always busy, managing both the children and the cooking. She picked the piece of cake up in her hands and took a bite. The moist dessert crumbled in her mouth with a delightful flavor. A warm feeling, like the glow from inside her family's cottage, began to grow in her chest. Taking the flask, she unscrewed the top. Haniah anticipated the refreshing taste of the water that came from the well by her home. If ever there was a time she could use some magic water, it was now.

She remembered Nuwairah's comment to drink deeply, so she raised the flask to her lips and took a big gulp. Rather than having a mouthful of cool well water, what she tasted was milk. It was the milk she had drawn from the cow. It was cool and sweet on the tongue. The taste of both the milk and cinnamon together was a familiar sensation, one she remembered from sitting and enjoying her family's company. Like white-capped waves heading for a troubled shore, she broke. At first it was a single tear, but gradually more came. She thought of her mother's touch, her father's smile, and her brother's voice. How good her life had been at home on the farm. She cried more. She cried into her hands and her chest began to heave.

Quiet sobs could be heard coming far from somewhere down the Gold Road, in the sunlight of the afternoon. Concealed from view under the tree, Haniah sat and drank deeply.

CHAPTER 6

The Inn and the Seeker

Stone Bridge was like many of the villages that dotted the countryside, with only one dirt road that ran through the entire town. The Gold Road was lined on either side with a sparse accumulation of buildings. These painted wood buildings rested on stone foundations cut from the surrounding hills. There was a mill where both grain was worked and lumber was sawn, and the barber shop doubled as a feed store. There were places of produce, an inn, and several cottages.

A healthy stream filled with trout and other fish bubbled through the east side of town. A hefty stone bridge crossed the water and welcomed visitors to the appropriately named location.

In the center of the village was a clearing the locals called the village square. A pole had been erected in the center of a stone alter that sat in the center of the clearing. A bright red sign was attached to the pole with "Gathbiyya" written in flourishing calligraphy and an arrow pointing east, and "Storm Sea" written below with an arrow pointing west.

Not much happened in this town and certainly nothing of historical value. There was commerce and travelers who stopped for the night, but it was not what one would call a destination. Those who came also went without much disruption. It was quiet, and the few people who lived there liked it that way.

By the time Haniah had wandered into the outskirts of the town, the sun had set low on the horizon. The day was turning into dusk and all those about were working on finishing their business so they could turn in for the night. Her feet were covered in dust and her legs were tired. She had pushed herself the last few hours, not wanting to get caught in the dark.

A woman on the road passed by Haniah on her way to a home across the street. She kept a shawl over her head and did not pay any attention to the girl walking the street into town.

She walked past a stray, yellow dog and up to a cart filled with red and yellow peppers. At the sight of food, her thoughts turned to her hungry belly. Walking all day with only a piece of cake to assuage her afternoon hunger had left her famished. She was running low on energy. Her mouth watered for a bite of the vegetables.

"Can I help you?" asked a woman who had been sitting next to the cart. The unpleasant tone shook Haniah from her focus. She saw a wrinkled and haggard woman with a pointy nose and a mole precariously placed on her right cheek.

"Yes. I am hungry and I was wondering how much your peppers are," said Haniah.

"That depends on how much you have?" The woman stood with one hand on the tall wheel attached to the cart.

"I don't have any money," confessed Haniah. "Maybe I could have just one of your peppers and I could pay you back?"

"No money, no peppers!" The woman scoffed. The woman was about to send Haniah on her way before she laid a greedy eye on the locket around Haniah's neck. "We may be able to make a trade though," said the woman, raising her hand in an attempt to touch the necklace.

Haniah instinctively grabbed the silver disk and tucked it behind her shirt. "I have nothing to trade. My family's farm was attacked last—"

"No money, no peppers!" The woman cut Haniah off before she could finish her sentence, upset that Haniah had hidden the polished silver. "Now off with you and stop bothering me." She waved her hand vigorously, shooing Haniah down the road.

Further down the road, past a home with its shutters already closed for the coming night, was a brightly painted wagon. It was a high-sided wagon with shelving and doors that opened to the side to display a variety of goods for sale. Among the many different items were finely made decorative knives, a game board made of marble rock, and a few books bound in various types of covers. A mule stood unhitched, grazing on a patch of grass tied beside it. The peddler of the traveling shop bustled about, checking his inventory. Haniah stood in front of the shelves, looking at the selection of new books and thinking of her father. The peddler looked out from behind the wagon as Haniah selected a copy of a book titled *To Forever and Back*. She opened its pages and looked at the printed words. She held the book to her nose and enjoyed the new book smell, just as she would when her father brought her a gift.

"Well, are you going to buy something or just look?" asked the man.

His hair was slicked back with oil, and he twisted a long mustache with his fingers. He wore a tailored suit that had seen better days. The pants were faded and the colorful tie tucked into his vest was fraying at its ends.

"I was just looking, sir," said Haniah, placing the book back. "I have no money."

The man spat to the side. "No money? You must have money to buy from me, girl," the man clamored. "I want riches, money, gold, and silver. Whatever you have. Have you none of those things?"

"Not to sell, sir." Haniah spoke in her kindest voice.

"Then you're no good to me," said the peddler.

Haniah's shoulders slumped. Never in her life had she been spoken to so unkindly. She had entered town expecting to find people who were friendly and kind. So far all she had found was a group of people who were greedy. Haniah pushed her feelings down, not allowing the man the satisfaction of seeing her cry. She stood there looking him sternly in the face.

"Well, if you're not going to buy then run along and don't waste my time." He gave her a harsh nudge with his hand. "Now go." Haniah resisted the push with her weight and walked away on her own.

Dejected, Haniah next approached the mill. A man worked, unloading a wagon that had been backed into a platform under the cover of an overhanging roof. A second man in overalls rolled up past his ankles stood on the dock, periodically making checkmarks. He held a board, keeping track of numbers as casks of pickles were unloaded. Haniah walked to the side of the wagon and looked up to see a man she recognized doing the counting. It was Mr. Halford, the man her father sold their wool to each year. He was the primary tradesman in town. He dealt in goods grown and raised from around the area.

"Excuse me, sir." Haniah waved to get his attention.

The man turned from his bookkeeping and eyed the girl who had spoken. "Yes? Do I know you, young lady?" he asked.

"Yes, Mr. Halford. My name is Haniah," she said. "You know my father, Fadi. He has been taken. Along with the rest of my family."

He thought for a moment, placing his pen to his chin. "I know your father," said the man. "He tried to cheat me." He spoke bitterly and now looked at Haniah with distaste. "Your father is a scoundrel."

"You must be thinking of someone else," said Haniah. "My father is a kind and fair man."

"I speak of Fadi," said the man. "He wanted to rob me."

"How so, sir?" asked Haniah, not liking how the man spoke of her father.

The second man stopped rolling barrels for the moment to listen.

"He wanted me to pay outrageous prices for his wool," said the slender man in overalls.

"I am sure it was the same price or similar to what he asked last year," said Haniah.

"Yeah, well times have changed," grumbled the tradesman. "His wool isn't worth what it used to be. Now that the capital is trading in some fashion called silks and satins." He waived his hand and pointed. "Now move along before I call and have you removed."

Haniah saw that it was pointless to reason with the man. His heart was hardened. She turned to walk away.

"Who was that?" Haniah overheard the man hauling the pickles ask.

"Just an urchin from down the road," said Mr. Halford.

"At least she isn't another one of those seeker types that have been passing through these parts lately," said the pickle man as he turned to rolling crates again.

Haniah walked the dusty road with her head down. The people of Stone Bridge had changed since she had visited. They were no longer kind, open people.

The hearts of men are beginning to fail. The words spoken by her father at the well whispered in her memory. She fingered the chain around her neck and pulled out what she had hidden. Standing in the village square under the red and yellow sign, she opened the locket. The blue glass glowed. The picture of the wizardess was gone. The green arrow was dimly lit and pointed to her left. She turned to face where the arrow pointed and its light grew brighter. She took a step in the direction she faced. The green light grew even brighter. She walked until she reached the wooden steps of a building. All the while, the little green light increased.

She stood at the base of six wooden steps of the village inn. It was a three story building with brightly colored shutters on every floor. Four gabled windows lined the top of the building. Over the years it had been painted several colors, but now had a dark blue coating. A porch ran the length of its front and around the sides. Decorative slats of wood lined its railing.

A wooden sign held by iron links hung high above the front door and marked the name of the inn, "The Wandering Goat." Haniah closed the compass and let it rest under her shirt. She placed her foot upon the first step and began to climb the stairs.

The door beneath the sign was open and led into a darkened room. The smell of pipe smoke and mutton filled the doorway. Steeling her nerves, she stepped forward over the entryway's threshold and into a place that opened up to reveal a common room filled with tables and chairs. Large beams held up the ceiling above and wooden poles stood to bear the weight of the beams. The lanterns did little to brighten the dim surroundings.

At a table in the middle of the room, two men and a woman sat with plates of food and drinks. Wearing the traditional wool clothing of locals, they sat huddled together, talking. At another table in the corner were men jesting and playing at cards. There were more empty chairs than there were filled. Along the wall was a row of tables separated by high-backed boards making private booths. A small pop of sparks sprung from the fire burning in the hearth.

"Who are you?" came a rough voice from behind the bar. Haniah looked to see a large man wearing a soiled apron approaching her. He came to rest in front of her, his frame looming. "Well, speak up."

"I am Haniah," she said. "I have walked all day to get here. My family is in danger and I have come to find someone to help me."

He placed his hands on his big belly and looked around the room. "At this moment we don't have any vigilantes in the inn and the king's men haven't passed through these parts for many summers," said the man. "What we do have is good cooking and rooms for rent."

"Then maybe I can get a room to stay in for the night?" asked Haniah.

"Do you have any money?"

"No."

"There is no charity here." He laughed heartily and turned to a waitress bustling about the tables. "Did you hear that? This girl wants a room, but has no money." Grabbing her by the shoulders, he turned Haniah around and began to push her from the room. Haniah ducked under his grasp and moved next to the door where an armory of old weapons was piled in an old cask. Haniah grabbed a hilt and pulled an old dilapidated sword from the tangle of blades. Backing against the wall she raised the blade between her and the man.

"Well, now. I wasn't expecting that," said the man with amusement in his voice. He raised his hands and stood his ground. "Do you even know how to use that?"

"I am not leaving here until I find someone who can help save my family." She spoke with as much firmness as possible. Her legs shook and felt like they would give out from under her. She lifted the sword in an attempt to keep the man from seeing her fear. "My family was attacked by goblins."

Upon hearing the word goblins, the occupants eating their supper stopped to look at the two.

"Goblins? I think you have been listening to too many stories," said the innkeeper, taking a step closer to the blade. "There are no such things as goblins."

Haniah retreated by sliding down the wall and into the pile of weapons.

"Are you a runaway? Is that it?"

"Don't come any closer," said Haniah, the sword shaking in her hands.

"You couldn't use that sword to save your life," said the man with a laugh.

Haniah jumped when a towering figure lumbered into the corner of her sight. "Come now, she's just a girl," said the newcomer. His voice was deep and hummed with base. She did not turn her attention from the hovering innkeeper to see who spoke.

"I guess you're right," said the innkeeper, taking a step back.

The large body of the newcomer moved in front of her. "There is no need to escalate this to where there is an accident." The voice spoke to her in a gentle tone. "Please, won't you put the sword down?" The words seemed to vibrate the air around her.

Loosening her grip on the hilt, color entered back into her knuckles. The tip of the sword lowered to the ground. She looked up to see a broad-headed beast towering over her. His forehead had a long crease that ran the entirety of its length. It was not a forehead that read surprise, curiosity, or alarm, but rather it was a forehead that indicated all three at once.

She stared, having a hard time deciding whether or not she was look-ing into the face of a great bear. Its ears were pulled back behind a head of blue fur. A pair of glass spectacles rested above a black, wet nose the size of an apple. She had seen a couple of bears before in the hills near her home, but not so close up.

But this was not a bear. It was something different entirely. He wore a coat with pockets and a pair of trousers tucked neatly into boots.

"She can sit with me," said the beast. He stepped aside and raised an arm to lead the way for Haniah to pass.

Haniah timidly walked by.

"Fine, she can sit with you," said the innkeeper, watching Haniah move toward a booth along the wall. She still carried the sword. "You can keep the old sword. It's just taking up space. Besides, it's so rusty it will never be good enough to reflect the light again." He pulled a wash towel from his hip and turned back to the bar.

"Right here." The bearlike creature motioned for her to take a seat at an empty booth. On the table sat a mug.

She removed her satchel and set it beside her as she slid into the bench. The creature took the seat across from her. She stared wide-eyed at the blue face. "What are you?"

"I am a Huggar," he said. "I can see from the look on your face you have never seen one such as I."

She shook her head. "No, not exactly. But there are a lot of things lately I have never seen that I am seeing for the first time."

"I come from Huggar," said the beast. "What you may refer to as the North Kingdom. We do not travel these parts much anymore." He took a sip from his cup. "Excuse my manners." He placed the cup to the side. "My name is Barir." He paused for a response.

Haniah sat in shock at seeing a beast talk so cordially, as if she should think it nothing out of the ordinary. He raised a furry eye brow at her delay. "Do you have a name?"

"My name?" she stammered. "My name is Haniah." A trickle of questions seeped into her head. "What brings you here?"

"I am a seeker," he said. "I seek the Gems of Anwar. I have traveled many days to arrive here. Are you from around here?"

"Yes, about a day's journey to the west."

"Oh, good. I don't have a map of the area. But someone like you might be able to help." He began to dig through a pocket on his coat. "Would you happen to know where there is a well to draw water from around these parts?"

"Why would you want a well?" asked Haniah, suddenly suspicious after having been attacked at it the night before. She did not trust this newcomer to share this information.

He pulled from his pocket a handful of crumpled pieces of paper and began to sort them on the table. "Ah, here it is," he said, lifting one piece of wrinkled paper between thick fingers. "I have it in my notes that the first gem will be found near a well of water."

"Where did you get that information?" asked Haniah, even more suspicious now.

"I have read and studied about the Prophecies of the Gems for many seasons," said Barir. "It is for this reason I have come. I believe one of the gems was found last night."

"How do you know this?"

"If you would join me at my camp, I can show you," he said.

Haniah thought for a moment. Her luck in finding someone in town to help her had thus far proven fruitless. The wizardess who had saved her said she needed to find the gems to save her family. Though she had not found anyone who was interested in helping find her family, this was the first per...er...thing to be interested in finding gems. That, in the end, might help her find her family. "Ok, I'll go to your camp with you," she said.

"Good," he said with a pleasing smile. "Tell me. Is what the innkeeper said true? Are you a runaway?"

"No," she said, not giving any more information. She did not know if this Huggar beast was something that could be trusted.

"Good. I would not wish to help someone run away whose parents were missing them." He pulled from his waist a small pouch and took from it one copper piece and placed it on the table.

"An entire copper piece for a drink?" she asked in amazement. "That's enough for my mother to make five entire meals for my family, and then some."

"I do okay where I come from." Barir retied the sack to his belt. "But I would agree, things are expensive and hard to come by here. Especially good company." With those words, he smiled and slid out from behind the table. Haniah grabbed her bag and sword.

They passed those eating supper without attracting any notice from them or the innkeeper. She followed him out the front door and down the wooden steps. The sun had set. She pulled the compass from out of her shirt and opened it. In the glass circle was an image of the big blue beast and his grin. The green arrow lit bright, pointing directly at the back of her new found companion, Barir.

"You're the second nicest person I have met today," said Haniah tucking the locket away. "May I call you a person?"

"Sure. You can call me a person, a Huggar, or Barir," he said in his deep voice. "Some of that has to do with the prophecies. I have noticed many of the human's hearts in this land have hardened. The good thing is, I am not a human." He looked over his shoulder. "Would you have used that sword on the man in the inn?" he asked.

"I don't know. Maybe if he had grabbed me."

The beast grunted in displeasure.

"Wouldn't you have done the same?" she asked.

"No," said Barir.

"Why not?"

"I'm a pacifist."

"A pasa…What?" asked Haniah.

"A pacifist," said the Beast. "A pacifist does not resort to violence."

"How can you be a seeker and not fight?" she asked aghast.

"I did not say I do not fight. I said I do not resort to violence."

Haniah walked behind, trying to puzzle out his words. "How can you fight and not be violent?"

"There are other ways of showing your will without physically harming someone."

"I have something bad after me. You might not want to be around me if you can't protect yourself," she said.

"There are many things I am, but a coward is not one of them." Haniah's parents had taught her to be wary of strangers. Now she was following one to his camp. A faint feeling of guilt crept into her chest. She did not wish to betray the lessons her parents had taught, but she saw no other option at hand. The world she once believed in had now changed. Her guilt turned to fear. Would she have to change as well?

CHAPTER 7

Three Stars

Barir's camp was on a hill above the village, nestled within a group of trees. His sleeping roll was on a pack filled with provisions. He had started a fire and had a pot of vegetable stew brewing in the flames. Haniah's mouth watered as the scent of the onions being chopped and placed in the pot reached her nose. It had been several hours since she last ate, and the beast's offer to share made him all the more likable.

Under a blanket of darkness, they sat—she on a cut stump and he on a rock. Haniah sat closest to the fire. She liked how it kept out the dark from the forest.

"You don't like the dark, do you?" asked Barir.

"No, not really," replied Haniah.

"I noticed the stars fading late last season," he said. "Many in my home land hardly noticed. We have so many lights coming from our cities that they drown out the light of the stars." He paused to look up. "That is one reason I seek the gems. I miss the stars."

"That must be a big city. Are there a lot of people like you where you come from?"

"Yes. In the North Kingdom there are many Huggars," said the beast.

"How did you notice the stars when others didn't?" asked Haniah as she poked at the fire with a stick.

"I have always been fascinated with the sky." He stirred the stew with a long, wooden spoon. "When we are young, we are given tests to see what we are interested in and good at. My evaluation showed I was strong in faith, so I was sent to school to study the heavens."

"Sent to school?"

"Yes, in my land we have institutions of learning. We have buildings made specifically for study, and there are Huggars trained to teach specific subjects," said Barir.

"My mother teaches me at home," said Haniah, interested. "What other things do they teach?"

"Well, almost everything." He walked over to his backpack. He pulled from the pack a long, bronze tube with metal gearing and poles attached to it. "There is philosophy, writing, smithing, mathematics, magic. Just about anything. My chosen field of study is astronomy." Barir returned to the fire. "There are many things we do not know about the stars. Some people speculate that stars are our ancestors. They say they look down upon us at night. Others believe they are a product of something called fusion, where tiny little particles of magic are fused together to create heat." He looked at her with a twinkle in his eye. "Some people think we are all created out of star dust."

"What do you believe we are created from?" asked Haniah.

He caressed the bronze tube in his arms. "I believe I am an accumulation of all my life's experiences," said Barir.

"What does that mean?"

"It means that everything I have done in the past, the experiences I will have in the future, and what happens at this very moment all shape and mold me into who I am," said Barir. "My personality, my emotions, my hopes and dreams are all molded by my experiences."

"That's an interesting thought," said Haniah. "My mother says I am what I eat. She tries to make me eat broccoli. Does that make me a vegetable?"

Barir let out a deep laugh. "Yes, I am probably made out of a bit of broccoli too." He walked a little distance from the fire's light and worked with the contraption he had in his hands. The bronze tube sat on three long legs and reflected the light from the dancing fire.

"What is that?" asked Haniah, walking to Barir's side.

"A looking glass, used for looking at the stars," said Barir. He squinted one eye and placed the other into one end of the tube.

"What are you looking at?" questioned Haniah.

"The three stars that appeared the night before." He turned a knob that lowered the looking glass. "Please, have a look for yourself." He stepped to the side.

Haniah peered into a glass lens and saw three sparkling lights surrounded by black. She raised her head from the glass and looked at the spot in the sky where the device was pointed. In the distance, she could faintly make out the stars. She placed her eye back up to the looking glass and the stars jumped out again. "Is it magic?" she asked.

"I guess it could be considered magic by some," said Barir. "I like to think so. But I am biased in my opinion." He placed a finger beside his nose. "The three stars are a sign that a stone has been found and used."

"How do you know this?" she asked.

"Because I have read it." Haniah followed as they walked to his backpack, now leaning against a branch. He pulled from it a thick book with a deep crimson cover. It was nicely bound in leather with gold leafing on the edge of its pages. He sat and thumbed through the pages of the book to one of many strings that hung from its pages and acted as bookmarks.

"What is that?" asked Haniah.

"It is a book of the prophecies of Anwar as dictated by the hand of Julie Jordan," he said, placing his hand on an open page. "The only copy known to exist after the burning of Assima." The book looked large, even in the Huggar's giant hands. "There it is." He marked the passage with the point of his finger.

A Gem shall be given in the night when they are captured;
One will escape, saved by the lady clothed in white.
Then shall appear in the sky three stars to mark their fate.

Haniah listened and pondered its significance. She was given a gem by her father the night before. She did see a woman clothed in white. A white light, to be more precise. Her family was attacked. Could the prophecy possibly be talking about her experiences?

She looked back up at the three distant stars. *The stars mark their fate.* A series of questions formed in her mind. Could it be that her father, mother, and brother all looked down on her now? Trapped in the sky? This was the first night she had noticed any new stars. More importantly, if they were trapped in the sky, could they be saved?

"Do you believe our ancestors are the stars?"

"I don't discount anything being possible." Barir noticed her looking intently into the sky. "These three stars seem to defy the darkness. Almost as if they were challenging it." He looked over to Haniah to see if she had anything to add. "What was it you said at the inn about your family being attacked by goblins?" he asked.

"My family was captured by something evil last night," she said. "I have to find the gems to save them."

"That is interesting," he said scratching a furry chin with his hand. "I would not have thought goblins would have been able to enter the kingdom. Though if they could, I would not put it past them to try to obtain the gems for themselves." He looked down at her. "You plan on finding these gems?"

"Yes." She said. "Maybe we can help each other. Once I have saved my family you're welcome to the gems. You can have them. I just want my family back."

He thought for a moment. "I have the book of prophecies and knowledge. What do you have to offer if we enter into an agreement and seek the gems together?"

Haniah moved to pick up her satchel. Barir closed his book and directed his attention to the girl. She untied the rope that kept it closed and pulled from the bag a brilliant white gem. She held it out to the beast. Barir placed his book to the side as he lowered himself to one knee, dropped his head, and bowed before her.

"You're a guardian," he said in reverence, without raising his head.

Haniah was surprised to see his response and pulled the stone close to her body. "You can stand up."

He lifted himself to his feet with the aid of the rock he had been sitting on. "Where did you get that?" he asked.

"My father gave it to me." She reached back into the bag and pulled from it a folded piece of parchment. "He also gave me a map."

"Why didn't you tell me you had these things?" asked the beast with interest.

"I didn't know if I could trust you, and I didn't want you to take them from me," she said.

"I can't do that," he said. "It could only be used for evil if I were to take it by force." He took a seat on the rock again. "Besides, I'm a pacifist." He gave her a long, exaggerated wink. "Remember?"

She nodded, her heart swelling with hope. Haniah looked the beast squarely in the eye. "So, it's a deal?" she asked.

"Yes, it's a deal. We will find the gems together." He rubbed his chin with the back of his hand.

"What else does it say in that book of yours?" asked Haniah.

"The gems are Elver-made," said Barir, thumbing through its pages. "Many summers ago, long before you or I were born, and before the three kingdoms were unified, there lived an Elver princess named Anwar. One day, while walking through the woods, she met a prince. A human prince. They became friends and met regularly at their favorite oak tree. There they shared their most sincere desires and whispered secrets to one another."

Haniah leaned in, fascinated by the story. "Over time, they fell in love," Barir continued. "But her parents did not approve of her choice. The Elvers are an ancient race who occupied the land long before the humans, and they believed it was a disgrace to associate with the newcomers. The humans were wary of the Elvers' queer ways and treated them likewise. Because of the disdain between the races, a darkness fell upon the land, and the two races went to war. This is known as the Dark War."

"I've heard of that," Haniah interrupted.

Barir nodded. "In secret, the Elver princess married the Human prince. Both kings and queens on either side died during the war, making the Prince and Princess Anwar as King and Queen of two warring nations. Although both immediately ended the war, the influence of the darkness was so strong that they could not restore order to their people. During this time of despair, other evils began to creep into the kingdoms and threatened the lives of both the King and Queen. To save her husband, Queen Anwar gave her soul to create the gems as a protection for her King. With the gems' power, the King was able to defeat the darkness, but at a great price. He had lost his love. The gems I speak of are the very gems we seek."

"What happened to the people and the King?" asked Haniah.

"The people stopped their war and have lived in peace. Until now." said Barir. "The King was not alone. Anwar bore his son, the heir to the kingdom. Their posterity have ruled the West Kingdom for the last three hundred years."

"So the King of the West Kingdom today has an ancestor who was an Elver Queen?" asked Haniah, piecing the story together in her head.

"Yes," said Barir.

"And where does the King live?" asked Haniah.

"The King lives in the capital city of Gathbiyya."

"I met a woman once who said she was searching for the King," said Haniah.

"Why, is he missing?"

"I don't know," said Haniah.

"I don't know either. But then, I have had such little interaction with this part of the human world. Can I look at the map?"

"Sure." She handed the folded map to him and placed the gem back in its bag. He carefully unfolded the map. He scooted to one side of the rock to let her sit next to him. Together they looked at the map with its shimmering ink.

"I can read some of this," he said, looking at the foreign script. After taking some time to decipher the slanted writing, he continued, "It is Elver writing. It says it is a map that shows the locations of the four Gems that have been placed around the kingdom." He pointed to the West Hills. "Here we are. It says in this writing that the White Gem is located at the Well of Aini." He pointed to some lettering Haniah could not make out. Turning his attention from the map he spoke to Haniah. "Is that where your gem came from?"

"Yes, my father pulled it from the well by our farm."

"Then there are three gems left." He searched the map, his finger running along its surface. "According to this map, the closest one to us is located in the Mountains of Hayud on the northern border." He pointed to some writing next to a picture of a staircase and read, *Climb the Stairs of Jabal. Here lies the Blue Gem.*"

"I guess we know where we are going," said Haniah.

"That we do. To the Stairs of Jabal!" Haniah's stomach grumbled. Barir noticed. "You must be starving. I think the stew is ready."

He folded the map and handed it back to Haniah. She placed it in the satchel. He poured a cup of stew into a bowl, placed a spoon inside, and handed it to the hungry girl. She ate like the pigs back on her farm, taking bites entirely too big for her mouth. Stew poured from the corner of her lips back into the bowl she ate over. "This is good," she managed to say between two quick bites.

"I am glad you like it."

"Does your book say anything else about the four gems?" she asked, wiping stew from her chin with her sleeve.

"It does. Each gem is designated by its color." He picked up his book and opened it to a bookmarked page. He read,

> *"To the Golden Gem it is given*
> *White to light the way in darkness*
> *Blue to soothe the soul in time of sadness*
> *Green to grow courage true*
> *Red to burn the hearts anew."*

"What does that mean?" she asked as she scooped up the last of her soup from her bowl.

"Each of the gems are different," he said. "They grant powers to the one who holds them—powers that increase the individual's natural talents or skills. But these words of promise seem to speak specifically to one gem. I believe they refer to the blessings bestowed upon the one who finds the Golden Gem." He poured himself a bowl of stew. Haniah held out her bowl for seconds.

"What do you know about the Golden Gem?" she asked as he poured more stew into her bowl.

"I have read all the information we have about it. It is the fifth gem, only to be revealed after the first four are found. It is the Golden Gem that binds all power, which is granted to the one who finds it. It is this Golden Gem that will save the world."

"Does it say where to find it?" Haniah shifted her weight on the rock.

"There is no information on that," said Barir, taking a taste of his stew. "We will have to worry about the four gems for now. What…" Barir's ears twitched and he peered into the darkness. "Someone is coming." He sniffed the air. "And they aren't human." He threw down his bowl and picked up his book. "Hurry, we must hide." Haniah grabbed her satchel and began to follow him into the brush. She quickly turned around, ran over to the fallen branch where her sword lay, and picked it up. She ran to his side and followed him into the dark. Concealed by a bush, they stopped at a point where they could make out the fire still burning.

Into the camp crawled two grotesque goblins. Their skin looked singed with soot and blisters where it peeked through their leather armor. One carried a wicked club riddled with spikes and the other a sword. The one with the sword had an ear that was disfigured, as though a bite had been taken out of it. The one with the club had a scar that ran from its left ear to the bottom of its chin. They came pushing and grunting, one nearly tripping over the other. "Watch where you're going," snarled the one with the sword, giving the other a shove with its fist.

"You stink," barked the other, pointing its club accusingly.

"No. You stink!"

"You both reek of putrid smells," said a third, who pushed his way through the first two. He was only about the size of Haniah, not nearly as big as the other two. Where the others wore armor, this newcomer had only a loin cloth. Also unlike the larger creatures, his limbs were thin and sinewy. He gripped a serrated knife in his fist. Like the others, he had razors for teeth and blood red eyes. He walked hunched over through the camp, twisting his head to the left and to the right. "Being stuck with you two on these search parties is enough to make me want to pluck out my own eyes. It's a wonder I can smell it at all with you two around."

"Is it here?" asked the one with the bitten ear.

"Oh yes." The creature let the "s" linger on its lips. Its voice simmered in a sinister speech that made Haniah cringe. Barir placed a soft hand on her shoulder. "I can smell it, and from the looks of things, it was here not too long ago."

The two goblins walked to the fire. The one with half an ear looked into the pot. He placed a finger in the stew, lifted it out, and licked it. "Eeeh! Herbs and vegetables." It knocked the pot over in anger. The stew spilled out into the fire.

"I am so hungry, I could eat a horse," said the one with the scar.

"Yeah? I could eat all the humans in that village we passed and still be hungry," the one with the marked ear bragged.

"No, you couldn't!" said his companion, baring its teeth. "I am far more hungry than you."

"No, you're not!" screamed the goblin as it thrust its weight into the other, knocking both to the ground. They rolled in the dirt, kicking and biting.

"Stop it or I'll hang both your heads on a pole," the smaller one said. In fear for their lives, the two arguing goblins complied. The leader sniffed the air. "Keep looking. It's somewhere around here."

Haniah's heart pounded in her ears. She thought it a wonder the goblins couldn't hear it trying to escape her chest.

One goblin walked to Barir's backpack and began to tear it apart with its clawed hands. It threw out cook wear, books, and clothes. It shredded the sleeping roll.

The second goblin grabbed the bronze cylinder of the looking glass and pounded it against the ground repeatedly. Barir watched mournfully from his hiding place. There was nothing he could do without revealing their location. The glass from the lens shattered. The legs on the tripod were beaten and bent until the thing lay in a tangled mess on the ground. Barir's eyes filled with silent tears.

The short one in charge crawled about on his hands and feet inspecting the garbage, looking for clues to where the campers had gone. "Come," said the creature. Together, the goblins departed in the same direction they had come, pushing and shoving.

Haniah and Barir sat quietly for what seemed like forever before she said anything. "That was close. What was that?"

"That was a witheram," said Barir in a low voice.

"Should we go get our stuff?"

"No. It's not safe. We will have to leave it." He stood up from behind the bush. "We should get as far away from here as possible, and as fast as we can." He took her hand and started jogging, heading away from the light of the dying campfire. Once a little distance away and out of hearing range of the goblins, they began to run. They ran till Haniah's legs grew tired and her breathing became labored. She carried the gem on her back and her sword in her hand. Barir had only his crimson-covered book and a bag full of coins. In the dark, they stopped and crouched down to the ground to catch their breath.

"Now what?" Haniah asked.

"We get the Blue Gem. On to the ice and snow of the Hayud Mountains."

CHAPTER 8

The Thief

THE OBELISKS WERE TALL. EVEN IF HANIAH WERE TO STAND ON Barir's shoulders, she would still not be able to touch the tops of the stone pillars that lay before them. They were in a meadow, surrounded by wild lulu flowers that Barir enjoyed eating. He held a handful of pink petals that he munched on periodically. Haniah had tried them, and though they were edible, they were a little too flowery for her taste.

They had traveled a week without any other incidents involving goblins or witheram. They stayed off frequently traveled roads or anywhere they might run into people who could pass along their whereabouts. They foraged for nuts and berries that they could eat as they walked. For the most part, they filled up on roots from pinker bushes that grew abundantly in the area. The white root left a tart aftertaste, with a texture similar to a potato. Barir carried a few in each of his pockets.

The night they saw the witheram, they ran as long and as hard as they could. Once Haniah had given over to exhaustion, Barir had picked her up and carried her. In his arms, she slept comfortably until sunrise. They covered more ground than they would have if she had kept running.

"They are Elver," said Barir studying the markings carved on one of the obelisk's sides. "They have left artifacts like this all around the land."

"Where are they now?" asked Haniah.

"They have all but left these parts and have confined themselves primarily to the East Kingdom." His attention still lingered on the obelisk.

The two towering structures stood side by side within a few long strides from one another. "This is the gateway of Gib. These stones distinguish the dividing line between the lands of the West Hills and the Mountains of Hayud." He placed a firm hand along the stone's weathered edge and ran his large hand down the side. "It's said to be good luck to pass through the gateway when walking from one region to the other."

"Well, I guess we should probably pass through them then," said Haniah decidedly. Standing between the obelisks, she held her breath and took a step forward. She crossed the threshold separating the Western Hills from the Hayud Mountain range. She had anticipated something special happening—a chill in the air, a sensation of magic—but nothing happened. She was just one step closer to a new destination and one step farther from her home. She breathed again. It dawned on her that she had never been so far from home. She had never imagined she would actually travel so far. It felt far. With every step, she wondered whether she was stepping closer to or farther away from her family.

A deer passed quietly along the border of the trees and the meadow. It stopped to look at the pair of travelers and then dropped its head to eat.

Barir followed Haniah through the gateway and bent down to inspect the ground. He placed a finger in an indentation in the soil. "Wolf tracks," he said, smelling some dirt he had picked up. "They have been here recently."

"Shouldn't we be going then?" asked Haniah nervously. "We don't want to get caught by wolves out here."

"This isn't the first set of tracks I have seen," said Barir. "I started seeing them when I first entered your land from the North Border." He dropped the dirt and wiped his hand on his pants as he stood. "I imagine they are spread throughout the land. We will just have to be careful."

He stood and continued in the direction they had been traveling for the past six days. In the distance, Haniah could see a mountain range covered in rock and snow climbing upwards from the horizon. Through the haze, she could see jagged peaks and steep slopes of ice. It was still another day's journey until they would reach the base. Together they took another step to close the distance.

⇛⇝

As the sun reached across the sky, the pair came upon a village, or something like a village. "Village" was the closest word Haniah could think of to call it. The buildings were round huts made of sticks with straw roofs. They were not permanent dwellings. Rather, these buildings could be picked up and carried about from one place to another.

The people were short with dark hair and dirty faces. There were not many of them, only a few families living together.

A woman washing laundry saw the two approaching and ducked inside the closest hut. When she emerged from behind a blanket-covered doorway, a short man followed. He wore brightly painted leather clothing. Reds and yellows decorated his hat and boots.

"Who are you and what do you want?" the man asked roughly. He held up his hands, insisting they stop where they were.

"I am Barir, and this is Haniah. We are travelers seeking a guide to take us into the mountains," Barir said, coming to a stop.

"We don't have any guides here," said the man. "You can go around." He did not smile, and he waved his hand, pointing them off in another direction.

"We have money," said Barir. "We will pay well for aid."

"How well?" asked the man. He leaned forward, displaying his hardened chin.

Barir untied the sack on his waist. He held it up and shook the jingling contents.

"Very well," said the greedy little man. "Come with me." He turned and escorted them into his hut. Barir pushed aside the blanket and ducked through the doorway. Inside, the ground was covered with beautifully woven rugs boasting colorful patterns of stars, stripes, and swirls. From ceiling to floor, similar rugs hung. In the center was a small coal fire used for cooking. The man, woman, Barir, and Haniah sat around the fire.

"My name is Hadi, and this is my wife Radwa," said the man, gesturing to the woman who sat at his side. "Now, why do you want to go to the mountain?"

"We seek passage to the Stairs of Jabal," said Barir. It was the location he had seen on the map given to Haniah.

"The stairway is high in the mountains," said the woman. Hadi gave her a glare, and she tightened her lips.

"The way is treacherous," said Hadi. "Even if we did make it, rumors say there lives a monster."

"What kind of monster?" inquired Haniah.

"I do not know." He scratched a hard, stubbly chin. "No one who has gone there has returned. It will cost you." He tapped a pointed finger on the carpet.

Barir pulled from his bag a silver coin and tossed it on the carpet in front of them.

"That won't get you halfway up the mountain, and you will need provisions," said Hadi, turning up his nose.

Barir reached back in his bag and pulled from it one gold coin. He placed it onto the carpet and pressed it firmly with his thumb. Haniah's eyes widened as he removed his hand to reveal the money. It sat on the carpet like a royal crown. The man and his wife both stopped fidgeting and held perfectly still. He paused with one hand reaching out to touch it. Barir gave a nod of his head as if to say the money was theirs.

The man picked up the gold coin and turned it over in his sweaty hands. His wife looked on jealously.

"We have a deal then." Barir tied his pouch onto his belt.

"What is it you seek for you to pay this price?" questioned the man as he picked up the silver and pocketed both the silver and gold.

"What I paid should be enough for you not to ask any more questions," said Barir, now getting to his feet. "Now, how about those provisions?"

The man took them from his hut and walked a path that ran through the huts. They left his wife behind. Playing children stopped what they were doing to look at the giant blue creature walking in their midst.

"What are you doing giving an entire gold piece to these people?" Haniah hissed quietly, leaning in close to Barir so only he could hear. "That could feed hundreds or buy…" she stammered in her search for words. "It could buy…I don't know what!"

"These nomads are the best mountain climbers around." He spoke with the same calm, consistent voice he always used. "They have traveled these mountains more than anyone. The price is worth it." He leaned closer to her. "Besides, what we seek is far more valuable."

"Do you really think there is a monster?"

"I am counting on there being a monster," he said earnestly. "It will most likely be the guardian of the gem. This is a good sign. It tells me there is most likely a stone up there. And if there is, we will get it."

Their hired guide took them to a hut, similar to all the others. Inside, leaning against the carpeted walls, were backpacks and sleeping rolls.

"This looks like your size." Hadi picked up a coat and handed it to Haniah. It was made of deer skin with a fur lined hood. He looked at Barir. "Do you need a coat?" he asked.

"I think the coat I am wearing will be fine," Barir said. "I'm also covered in fur. I could use a backpack though." The short man picked up the largest backpack in the room and handed it to Barir. Barir looked it over pleasingly. "Thank you."

The short man handed a pair of boots to Haniah and a rope with rigging to Barir. "You will need this where we are going," said Hadi. He looked back at the pile of supplies and pulled from it a couple of ice picks. "This should do."

"When do we start?" asked Barir.

"We will start first thing in the morning," said the man. "Tonight you can sleep in here." Without any other words he turned and left, letting the rug door flap close.

"He was sure grumpy," said Haniah

"Have you never met a dwarf before?" asked Barir.

"No, never."

"They can be a bit temperamental. But more so now with the way things are changing in the world." Barir unfolded a bed role.

Barir and Haniah made beds among the supplies. Haniah lay awake for a while, wondering how she had found herself in this strange place. She listened to the deep breaths from the beast sleeping next to her as she drifted off to sleep.

∾∾

Haniah found herself hanging to the side of a cliff, hands grabbing hold of an outcrop of rock just large enough for her fingers to grab. With one foot placed in a crevice, she frantically looked to where she could place her other foot.

"Ok, to your right by your knee is a ledge," said Barir. "See if you can lift your foot up to it." He stood twenty horses below her in the snow, giving her the location of ledges and crevices. Haniah lifted her foot and found the ledge. She placed her weight on her feet to give her arms a rest. "Good job. You're almost there," called Barir.

Haniah looked up to the top of the cliff, which was still another ten horses above her. Hadi, the guide, stood looking over the edge down at the pair. He had climbed up first and secured a rope to the top of the cliff that was tied to both Haniah and Barir. Haniah stood on tiptoes, stretching to find the next place to put her hands.

"You're going to have to jump to make the next handhold," said the dwarf.

Haniah could see it just out of her reach. It was a nub of rock that stuck out from the face of the cliff. "I can't do that!" she exclaimed. "It's too far, and I'll fall."

"You can do it," said Barir, giving her confidence. "I will catch you if you miss."

This was the third cliff face they had scaled with ropes and each one was getting harder. She had already slipped twice and had to be caught by Barir. Each time, she would fall a short distance and hit the wall with either her shoulder or her hip before the rope caught her. Each fall had left a bruise and confirmation that it was not something she wished to do again.

They had started their climb early in the morning and walked over snowy fields of ice to reach the first wall face. They climbed it with effort and again walked along miles of snow drifts. Higher and higher into the mountains they climbed. Haniah was grateful for the boots she had been given that kept her feet warm and dry.

The guide led the way, Haniah followed a few paces back, and Barir brought up the rear. Barir carried the large backpack that had been given to him by the guide. They followed in one another's footsteps and were tethered by a rope tied to each person's waist. Haniah pulled her locket from the coat and opened it. She pointed it at the back of the dwarf she followed but there was no green arrow pointing to Hadi. There was no blue glow, no picture like the one she had seen when the necklace was held near Barir. There was nothing. She closed the locket and placed it back in her coat. Whether it meant that the man did not have a pure heart or not, she did not know. Perhaps the locket doesn't work this high up in the mountains. Haniah did not have much time to think about it. She needed to focus on where she placed her next footstep. The ice crunched beneath her feet.

The snow beneath Barir's feet gave way with no warning. He quickly grabbed the edge to keep himself from falling into the pit that opened up beneath his dangling legs. Haniah was pulled to the ground by the rope tied between them. Hadi stabbed his ice pick into the icy snow to keep them from sliding any more than they already had. Haniah picked up the pick she had dropped and hit it into the ice next to her. She gripped the handle firmly.

"You're going to have to lift yourself up," said Hadi, not moving from where he lay. "We will try to hold our ground as best we can."

Barir looked beneath him into an icy blue abyss. He grit his teeth as he lifted his upper body onto the icy edge.

"Good," said Hadi, giving instruction. "Stay on your belly. It will disperse your weight. We don't want you making another hole like the one you're in."

Barir lifted his legs up out of the crevice and, on his tummy, crawled up next to where Haniah lay, gripping her ice pick. Haniah's breath came in quick, short gasps.

"Get up," said the dwarf to Barir and Haniah in a tone that lacked patience. After seeing she was getting no sympathy from their guide, Haniah found the strength to stand and took great care where she placed her next step.

It was now well past noon and Haniah was getting tired. Again she clung to a cliff wall, and now they wanted her to jump to her next hand hold. Clinging to the cliff wall, her heart raced as her arms began to give out.

"Focus, Haniah." Barir could see her fear taking shape on her face. "You can do this." Haniah bent her legs at the knees, focused her eyes on a small bump on the ledge and jumped. With her arms raised above her head, she reached for the handhold and got it. Her fingers tightened around the rock as she dangled in the air.

"Okay, there is a foothold there by your left foot!" exclaimed Barir. Haniah placed her foot in a crack in the wall and stabilized herself. With the hardest part of the cliff completed, Haniah was able to finish the climb without incident. She leaned back over the ledge to see Barir begin his climb up the rock wall. His height and long arms let him reach areas Haniah could not reach, helping him to climb twice as fast. Hadi held the rope that was tied to Barir.

Barir pulled himself up to stand beside the guide and Haniah. They stood on the ridge of the mountain, high above the surrounding lands. Haniah looked at the world around her. It went on forever into the distance.

"This is as far as I take you," said Hadi, turning to face the ridge line that ran for a league, up to the foot of a long stairway that climbed close to the peak of the mountain.

"The Stairs of Jabal," said Barir. His tone was deep and reverent.

"What is that?" Haniah pointed to a stone structure or building of some sorts carved out of the mountain at the top of the stairs.

"That is a fortress built a thousand years ago," said Barir. "It will be deserted."

Hadi leaned close to Barir.

With one swift motion, the man cut the bag of coins hanging on Barir's belt and cut the rope that was tied to Barir. Grabbing the end of the rope, he swung himself down the cliff wall they had just climbed. Barir turned around in time to see the man place the pouch in his pocket and start running away down the snow covered field. The rope on the cliff wall dropped to the ground.

"There he goes!" cried Haniah.

Barir watched the desperate thief run. "Aren't we going to go after him?" Haniah looked up to squint incredulously at the beast.

"No," said Barir. "If we go after him, we will not be able to get back up here without his help, and once we catch him—if we catch him—I doubt he will be very willing to help us anymore. He knows these mountains better than we do, and he has a good head start."

"But he stole from you," Haniah pled, pointing her finger down the mountain.

"Sometimes you have to let go of something, even something as valuable as gold, to achieve something of more worth." Barir turned away from the little man to face the rest of the climb. "For right now, that thing is finding the next gem."

"But he's a thief!" Haniah watched the man grow smaller and smaller as he ran. "We can't just let him get away," she protested.

"We are almost there. We will forgive him and move forward." He continued on, placing his foot in white, untouched snow. Haniah dropped her arm, turned to face Barir, and reluctantly followed.

CHAPTER 9

Dragon Fight

AT THE TOP OF THE STAIRS, HANIAH AND BARIR FACED AN ENOR-mous door carved into the side of the mountain. The doorway was made with thick beams of wood that were fastened together with black, iron clasps. There were no hinges on the door.

"I don't see a handle," observed Haniah, examining the stone wall that stood around the door.

"It's on the inside," said Barir. He walked up to the door, his backpack still on his back. "This is a defensive structure. They would not have put it on the outside."

"How are we going to get in?" asked Haniah.

"I'll lift." He squatted low to the ground, then squeezed the tips of his fingers under the door. With a groan, he straightened his back and strained his legs to lift the door to his knees. "Crawl under," he said, gritting his teeth. Seeing the effort on Barir's face Haniah scrambled through the opening on her hands and knees.

"I'm in," came Haniah's voice from under the door.

Barir let the door drop with a thud.

Haniah stood in the middle of darkness. Placing her ear against the large stone door she listened for any sound that might come from outside. Nothing. The door was too thick to hear the sounds of Barir. Hanniah took a deep breath, pushing down her fear of dark. With one hand upon the door she shuffled her feet along its length until she came to what felt like a wood lever. Pulling down on the lever, a clang sounded above her head and the door began to move. Into the air it climbed to reveal the light of day and Barir.

"I found this lever!" Haniah stood next to the wooden handle she had just pulled. It was connected to a chain that was part of a pulley system.

"Good job," Barir said. The hallway before them stretched into the mountain. Great stone pillars were carved out of the walls, and the ceilings soared high above them, meeting at the top in vaulted points. Light streamed in through strategically placed skylights that shone down onto statues lining the walls.

"What is this place?" asked Haniah.

"This is a Huggar defensive outpost," said Barir, "built on the border of the North Kingdom and the West Kingdom. It would have been used as a lookout point."

Haniah walked up to one of several towering stone statues. The statue was weathered around the edges, but a closer look revealed a robed Huggar wearing a crown.

"Who is this?" asked Haniah.

"That would be a Huggar king," said Barir. "It looks like it could be King Badri Khamun. It would have been carved when this place was built, back when we still had kings in our land."

"You don't have a king?" asked Haniah with surprise.

"We have not had a king for over five hundred years." Barir started his walk down the hall. "In my land the people rule themselves." Haniah moved from the statue and walked by his side. "We are free to make our own decisions, without having to look to a monarch."

They walked past the pillars and statues. The floor was a mosaic of large stone tiles with sparkles that shimmered a brilliant blue as they passed. They saw some places where the walls had been torn down, and there were areas of the floor that had caved in, revealing dark pits beneath. Large stone blocks lay strewn across the floor. The further they went into the mountain, the colder it got. Haniah could see her breath in the air. They continued to walk down the hall into a room adorned with faded, tattered tapestries that had once been colorful. Below the tapestries were doorways leading to other rooms.

They chose a doorway on the left and entered a room with many unrecognizable devices and contraptions. Some sat on stone tables. The larger ones sat on the floor.

Barir walked to a table holding several clay jars marked with symbols. Most had lids with an iron rod sticking out of the top. A copper wire ran between the jars that connected each of them to their own iron rod. Barir looked inside some of the jars with missing lids. In each of the jars was a copper cylinder and what looked like old juice stains. Barir scratched the top of his head as he read the inscriptions written on the clay jars.

"Can you read it?" asked Haniah, looking at the clay inscriptions.

"Yes," said Barir. "It is old Huggar writing. It says it is something called a Kahraba."

"What is that?" asked Haniah.

"I don't know," he said. "In your language, it would sound like 'battery'. Do you know what that means?"

"I don't." Haniah gave him a puzzled expression.

"It says it works with lightning." He read more, then shrugged his shoulders in dismay.

Haniah walked over to one of the devices sitting on a table. It was a box made of brass. On top of the box there were buttons lined in rows, and on each of the buttons was a single symbol. A brass disk attached to the box sat on its end. It was decorated with brass snowflakes. Flat, blue glass was set into the center of the disk. It reminded her of her locket, only bigger.

"What is this?" asked Haniah, pushing a few of the buttons.

"It's a magic device," said Barir, looking at the symbols on the buttons. "Those are Huggar letters." He touched the face of the glass. "I am not sure what it does."

"Magic?" repeated Haniah.

"Yes. Huggars have magic." Barir turned his attention to Haniah. "This is a room of magic, where Huggars study and research. This would have made an ideal location to discover and keep new magic secrets. It's far away from others and hard to get to." Haniah looked around the room at the assortment of magic devices. "Each race has their own magic," he continued. "Human magic deals with perception and reality—they warp time and play with light and illusion. They make things appear and disappear. Only a wizard or wizardess can wield human magic."

"How does one become a wizard or wizardess?" asked Haniah interested in the topic.

"A human either has magic or they don't. It's born in them. To become a wizard or wizardess, one must take sacred rites and make special promises."

"What are the other races' magic like?" questioned Haniah.

"Elver magic is said to focus on the spirit, or the soul, that runs through the universe," said Barir as he crossed to the center of the room. "Elver magic can make things grow and has the ability to strengthen or nurture what is living or part of nature." His attention was focused on a large contraption made up of gears and wires. In the center was a lattice work of copper wiring that stretched out like an erratic spider web. An iron pole ran from the web up through an opening in the ceiling and into the open air above.

"Huggar magic is revealed through devices like this." He tilted his head to the side and squinted his eyes at the tangle of wiring. "Whatever *this* is. Unlike the other forms of magic, Huggar magic can be used by anyone once they have a device and know how to use it." He turned his attention to Haniah, who stood next to him. "The device I have seen you wear around your neck is Huggar-made." Haniah placed her hand over her coat where the locket lay. "Can I ask what it does?"

"It can tell if a person has a pure heart," said Haniah with some hesitation.

"What does it say about me?" asked Barir.

"It says I can trust you," replied Haniah, turning one corner of her mouth up to reveal just a hint of a smile. She looked at him with big brown eyes.

"On my honor I will do my best to live up to that trust." Barir nodded his head solemnly.

They walked down another hallway that led into a large cavern where the walls were intricately carved with geometric shapes. It was a circular room with a high-domed ceiling that opened up to the sky above. Overhead they could see white, billowy clouds passing in front of a blue sky. The ceiling had crumbled to the floor long ago, leaving a mountain of debris.

On the pile of broken rock lay something that made Haniah's breath catch. It was sleeping, taking great breaths that made its chest rise and fall in rhythmic fashion. Brilliant silver scales ran from the top of its head to the tip of its muscular tail. They glistened in the light as it shifted to a more comfortable position. It wore a crown of pleated horns on its head and a pair of wings on its back.

"I think that's our monster," said Barir in a soft tone.

"You mean the guardian?" whispered Haniah, looking over the dragon. Barir walked forward. "What are you doing?" She raised her voice to a louder whisper.

"I am going to wake it up," said Barir. Haniah didn't think it was bravery that drove the Huggar forward, but could not for the life of her figure out what it was. She slowly shuffled her way farther into the room. She stopped several paces short of where Barir stood, next to the huge beast. He reached toward the dragon and tapped it on the nose.

The dragon came to life, raising his head and lifting himself up on his front legs. Barir and Haniah both moved back, warily keeping their eyes on the monster. Sharpened claws stretched and scratched on the rubble. Mighty wings unfurled as the magnificent creature rose up in the air above Barir. The dragon was not as large as Haniah would have expected, only a bit larger and taller than Barir. Despite his smaller stature, the dragon was still clearly a threat. She thought it could probably eat them both in just a few bites.

"Who wakes me from my sleep?" the dragon thundered.

"I am Barir, Seeker of the Gems of Anwar. I have come to respectfully ask for access to your gem."

"I am the guardian Shudun. You must prove you are worthy of the gem before I give it to you." The creature arched his back and straightened his neck to stretch before continuing. "Or you may attempt to take it from me. I warn you, either test may end your life." Haniah continued to move back slowly, pulling from her belt the rusty sword she wore at her side. Shudun transferred his attention to Haniah. His gaze pierced her to the core, and she stopped in her tracks. "Who are you? Why do you bring steel, and why do you look at me so?"

"I am Haniah," she said, lifting the sword slightly, but not enough to threaten the creature. "I bring a sword to protect myself. I wasn't expecting to see a dragon. I have never seen one before, and I would have expected a dragon to be larger. That is why I stare."

"You judge my size?" Shudun bellowed. He bared his teeth and flexed the muscles on his shoulders.

"I wouldn't have said that," said Barir, backing up a few more feet.

"It is true, there are larger of my kind," said the dragon. "I am a Dwarf Dragon. But do not let my stature fool you." His voice rumbled and shook the walls as he spoke. "I break stone and make mountains crumble. I'll crush your bones to powder before I am through with you. It is not the outward appearance that makes one grand, but the power of one's heart." The dragon stuck out its scale-covered underside. "My heart will give way before I see the likes of you two take the gem from me. Now be gone!" The dragon stepped and turned on the pile of rubble like a cat getting ready to bed. He looked for a comfortable place to position himself once again.

"I really must insist," said Barir, raising a hand to the dragon. "We need the gem. It's important."

"In that case, come take it from me." The dragon spread its wings and leaped to the stone ground where Barir stood. Barir held his position and braced himself for the impact. The dragon hit Barir with the back of its forearm and sent him rolling to the ground. The dragon swept around in a circle to see Barir stagger to his feet. Barir stood there. He did not move; he did not run. He stood with his hands at his sides and his feet together. He raised his chin and looked the dragon in the eye.

"Look out!" Haniah shouted. The dragon spun its masculine tail fiercely. Like a whip, the full impact of its tail rammed Barir square in the chest, sending him flying across the ground and landing in a cloud of dust and debris. He lay still.

Haniah screamed and the dragon turned on her. Overtaken by fear, she froze in place. The dragon raised a clawed hand and brought it down on the little girl. Haniah cowered her body into a ball, the sword pointing in the air. The dragon's claw came down with force, impaling itself on the sword. The dragon sprang back in pain, yanking the sword out of Hani-ah's hands. Haniah fell to the ground.

The dragon beat his wings and rose into the air. He frantically thrashed and wailed as he hit against the wall, the sword still in his foot. Flying to the roof, he hit his body against the ceiling. Stone fell with a deafening crash, trapping Shudun under the broken ceiling's weight. The dragon did not move.

Haniah ran to Barir's side. He was breathing. "Wake up," she said, shaking his shoulder. He opened his eyes, and Haniah let out a sigh of relief. He rolled over, letting out a moan of excruciating pain. He noticed the dragon on the ground, rose to his feet, and limped over to where the dragon lay. Shudun's breathing was labored. A stone slab lay on top of him, pinning his wings and neck to the ground.

"Will you kill me now?" asked Shudun, unable to move.

"Give me a hand, Haniah," said Barir, walking over to where the dragon lay. He bent down and grabbed hold of the debris, placing a shoulder into the stone.

"What are you doing?" asked Haniah.

"Saving him," said Barir.

"But he just tried to kill us!" exclaimed Haniah as she threw her arms in the air. "Now you want to save him?"

Barir let out a roar as he pushed with the force of twenty men. The slab slid to the side, freeing the dragon. The dragon staggered back on legs weakened from being trapped.

Haniah ran to pick up the sword that had been dislodged from the dragon's foot. She braced her feet under her and raised the sword until it pointed at the dragon.

"You have done well," said the dragon, climbing back up on the mountain of rubble. He spoke to Barir. "You have proven to be a worthy Seeker. I shall grant you the gem you seek."

"Be careful! It might be a trap," said Haniah.

"Come closer," spoke the dragon. "I grant you the gem, not because you have defeated me, nor because you saved me. It is because of the way you fought." The dragon bowed his head.

"He didn't fight," said Haniah, thinking the dragon was trying to lure them in. "I did. It was my sword who stabbed you."

"And it is good that it did," spoke the dragon. Haniah wrinkled her nose, unbelieving. "You see, I am a very sensitive dragon. Sensitive to sharp objects, and sensitive to emotions. Yes, your sword pierced me, but your friend's actions have touched me and created feelings within me that I have not felt for a very long time."

"A sensitive dragon?" scoffed Haniah, balking at the ridiculous notion. She looked for a tear but did not see one on the dragon. Never in any of her books had she ever read about a dragon with feelings.

"It is sensitivity that protects the gem," said the dragon.

"How does sensitivity guard the gem?" asked Haniah, determined to get to the bottom of the dragon's motives.

"The idea of defending the gems is not to hoard them nor to keep them for myself forever," said Shudun. "The purpose of a guardian is to ensure that the gems are kept safe with one who is worthy of being a guardian."

"What makes one worthy?" asked Haniah.

"They must be pure in heart," said Shudun. "My sensitivity ensures that I will find someone who is pure in heart and someone I can trust to pass it on to. To keep safe. My sensitivity does not ensure that I can fight or keep it from someone who would take it from me with force. If someone has those intentions, they will do it with or without my consent."

"I am glad we made it to you first then," said Barir.

"Your strength has served you well, Seeker Barir," said the dragon, unfurling its wings. He turned to the side and revealed a scale that was not actually a scale. It was the same size as the other scales surrounding it, but it shimmered a brilliant blue and made the silver scales around it shine even brighter. "Come, take it."

Barir limped over to the dragon and pulled from his side the Blue Gem. He held it up above his head to the open sky. "This is amazing. I can feel the power of the gem running through my body." The great Hug-gar rolled his shoulders and stretched. "The pain is gone."

"The gem will only make you stronger," said the dragon.

"I thank you for it," said Barir. "We must go now. Our journey is far from complete, and we have a long way to travel."

"Go your way in peace," said Shudun. He laid back down to rest. Barir placed the gem in his coat pocket and turned to leave.

Haniah stayed silent as they walked out the door and through the stone cavern, past the room with magic devices and down the hall lined with statues of kings. Haniah could feel anger swelling up in her.

"So, you really don't fight do you?" asked Haniah as they walked under the suspended wooden door at the top of the steep staircase. She stopped and waited for a response. She was so angry, she had fire in her eyes.

"It is not that I do not fight," Barir said, turning around to face her. "I do not use violence."

"You can't fight and not use violence," insisted Haniah.

"One does not need a sword to fight," he said calmly. "I fight for what is right and just. I prefer for my displays of defiance to be peaceful protests."

"What just happened in there did not seem peaceful to me!" she screamed.

"As long as I am not an aggressor, I am satisfied with my actions and the outcome."

"The outcome could have been both your death and mine." She could feel the heat in her voice as her blood boiled. "What's your strategy when you don't fight, to die? You can't be a guardian if you're dead." She turned from him and sat on a step with her arms tightly folded.

Barir slowly moved closer to her and took a seat beside her. She slid away from him and shielded her face with her shoulder.

"I am sorry, Haniah," said Barir with all sincerity. "I am only doing the best I can. Will you forgive me?" His tone was soft. There was silence between them for a moment.

"I forgive you," said Haniah, turning to reveal tears in her eyes. "I have had my family taken away from me. You're all I have right now." She wiped her nose with her sleeve. "I couldn't take it if I was left alone again."

"I hear you," said Barir.

"Then will you carry a sword and fight?"

"I cannot," Barir said as peaceably as he could. "Within all creatures there is the potential for goodness and greatness. Even if that greatness is buried deep within them, even if their heart is as dark as midnight, or they are as weak as a willow mouse, somewhere within them lies at least a glimmer of goodness, a desire to be better than they are. My willingness to endanger myself rather than carry a sword, my sacrifice, stirs up the glimmer they hold, giving it the chance to grow. When they see that I will not hurt them, their hearts soften and grow. When it grows, it consumes the mediocrity within and the creature is made new. So, you see. I do fight, but not with weapons."

"I think I understand," said Haniah.

"If I die, then all the more powerful my fight and supplication."

"What if the creature does not want its heart to change?"

"That is its choice. At least I have given it a chance."

"Well, it was the sword that saved us back there," Haniah said, giving her friend a smile.

"So it seems," said Barir grinning back, neither agreeing nor disagreeing with the girl's statement.

"Oh no," said Haniah, looking down the stairs and the mountain's ridge. In the distance, Haniah could see black figures climbing. "Goblins!"

Barir squinted in the same direction as Haniah. The sun was setting, and it was hard for him to see. "They must have followed us." They stood and ran back into the fortress. Barir pulled on the wooden lever next to the great door, but it did not move. "It's stuck." He pulled on the lever so hard that it broke off in his hands. "I guess I'm stronger than I realized. Let's get back to the dragon. There must be another way down from here." Together they ran to the dome room to find the dragon.

Shudun sat in the center of the room where they had left him. "We were followed, and we need a way out," said Barir.

"By who?" asked Shudun, sitting up.

"Goblins." Barir pointed the way they had come. "We saw about fifty of them, not far down the mountain."

"That is too many to take on with just the three of us," said the dragon. "And the stairs are the only way up."

"Can you fly us out of here?" asked Haniah, looking up at the opening in the ceiling.

"I am not large enough to carry you both," said the dragon regrettably. "I may be able to fly you out, but that would leave your friend behind."

"You take Haniah and fly away with her. I'll fend for myself," said Barir.

"No, I am not leaving you," said Haniah, clinging to Barir's arm.

"I have an idea," said Barir. "There might be something in the room with the magic devices that can help us. Shudun, we will take care of ourselves. I hope you will not be here when the goblins arrive."

"I do not plan on staying if what you say is true," said the dragon. He jumped into the air and beat his wings. Shudun flew up through the hole in the ceiling and perched on its edge. "Take care, you two." The dragon flew overhead and out of sight.

"We must hurry." Barir pulled Haniah by the hand and ran through the doorway. They ran into the room filled with magic devices. "I think

I saw something on this one here." He pointed to the contraption that looked like a great spider web. Haniah saw a brass placard nailed to its frame. "There! It says it's some kind of flying machine."

"What? I see no wings on it," said Haniah.

"Yes, yes," Barir said distantly, too many thoughts running through his mind. "If I can just get it to work, it might take us away from here." Barir turned a crank attached to the spindle of wire. "Go grab hold of that web." Haniah did as he said. Faster and faster he spun the crank until the spindle began to make a crackling sound. They could both feel the hair on their heads standing on end. The clouds overhead accumulated around the iron pole that ran up through the roof. With the crank frantically spinning on its own, Barir moved to stand next to Haniah and grabbed hold of the copper webbing. "Hold on!" He raised his voice above the whizzing sound coming from the now spinning crank.

A flash of lighting struck the top of the pole and sent a charge down to the device. One moment, Barir and Haniah stood in the middle of the magic room with hands on the contraption, the next moment, they were gone, riding on a bolt of lightning.

CHAPTER 10

Fairy Circle of Tricks

HANIAH AND BARIR NOW OCCUPIED A ROOM SIMILAR TO THE ONE they had just left, only smaller and without all the magic devices. Haniah had felt a shock in her hand and saw a flash from behind her closed eyelids. When she opened her eyes, she was standing here.

"What just happened?" asked Haniah as she looked wide-eyed around the room. It was still cold and she could see her breath.

"I'm not sure, but it appears that the device has carried us to this location." They walked through a doorway and out into cool mountain air. They stood high up on a mountainside. The sun had not yet set here, and they could see the land stretched out for a great distance before them. Further down the mountain, the snow stopped, and green fields turned into forest. The forest covered the entire land and had no end in sight.

"Where are we?" asked Haniah.

"My guess is that we are still somewhere along the Hayud Mountain range," said Barir. "We are a great distance to the east, as the sun is about to set. My guess is that these two Huggar installations were used to keep a lookout on the border. The magic device we just used would have let travelers transport messages back and forth instantaneously. We are near the Elver borders, and that's the Shahirah Forest." He pointed southeast. "We should be going." He started down the mountain.

"Do you think the goblins will follow us?" asked Haniah.

"I doubt they are smart enough to figure out how to use the traveling device," said Barir, taking broad strides to cover ground quickly. "But if they do figure it out, I don't want to be here when they arrive." Down, down they walked, off the mountain.

∾

"Are you sure we are going in the right direction?" Haniah looked at a rock that sat next to the path they were on. They walked under a canopy of robust branches that grew from trees six horses high. The trees were spread evenly over the rolling hills, and plants covered the ground. "We have been in these woods for two days now and I think we have passed that same rock twice now."

"What rock?" asked Barir, stopping and taking off his backpack.

"That one." She pointed to a rock set behind a thick whisper oak tree. "The one with the moss."

"How can you tell?" asked Barir. He took a seat on a rock next to the path. "They all look the same to me."

"It kind of looks like you," she said, tilting her head to the side. "But from this angle it looks like it could also be a chicken."

"You're telling me you think I resemble a chicken?" He chuckled, appreciating the joke.

"I am telling you that you resemble a rock." She smiled and took a seat on a nearby log. "We are going in circles."

"Can I see that map of yours again?" Haniah set her pack aside and handed the folded parchment to him. "We have the White Gem and the Blue Gem. That leaves the Green and Red Gems." He unfolded the map on his lap. "According to my book and this map, the Green Gem is in a tower four days more in that direction." He motioned to the south.

"Four more days? I'm going to get a blister." She had stopped wearing the heavy boots and had gone back to her regular shoes once they were out of the mountains. Her coat and boots had been far too warm to wear when not hiking in the snow. Barir carried them in his pack.

"I think now is a good time to take a short rest," said Barir, leaning back into an alcove of dirt and grass. "I am going to take a nap." He closed his eyes to rest.

"I guess I am okay with stopping for a little while." Haniah looked at him and stood back up. She pulled the rusty sword from her waist and

∾

gave it a clumsy wave in front of her face. She imagined striking at a goblin and missing as she swung the sword, off balance. Barir opened one eye to see what she was doing.

"I might have something to help shine that sword up." He sat forward and dug through the pockets of his backpack. He handed her a metal scrub brush and a jar with something in it. "It's usually used to clean pots, but it should get the rust off. You might as well make it look nice if you're going to carry it." Haniah sat with the sword on her lap. With a dab of cream from the jar, she began to scrub the blade. "Don't touch your eyes or skin with it," Barir warned. Haniah could see some of the rust begin to brush off.

"Don't you object to me fighting with it?" asked Haniah.

"No. I do not judge you," he said, resting his back against the grass. "We each choose the path that works best for us."

"I'll do what it takes to get my family back," said Haniah, seeing just a glimpse of a reflection in the blade.

"I know you will." He closed his eyes and fell asleep.

Scrubbing the sword took her mind back to the farm and her chores. She could hear the tune her father whistled while carving with his tools. He would often accompany her in the barn where they would work together. She remembered her mother teaching her to sew a sleeve onto a shirt. How she would love to see her brother again and talk about fishing. She would never argue with him again if she could only be with them. Fishing. It would sure be nice to eat a meal of fish cooked by her mother.

She wondered how long it had been since she last ate. She had been hungry for a few hours. She closed the jar, leaving it and the scrub on the rock. She set the sword next to her pack. Haniah looked over at the sleeping Barir. She could forage some food for them and bring it back by the time he woke up.

She crept away from the trail, past the rock with the moss, and into the woods. She looked for edible berries and leaves or roots they could boil. Over a hill, around a tree and out of sight, something flew past her. Just outside of the corner of her eye she caught a flicker like a dragonfly or beetle, but it swept behind a branch. Haniah followed to investigate. When she came around to the other side it was gone. She heard a high pitch sound come from behind, almost like a giggle. She spun around to see a creature the size of a mouse fluttering in the air. Its vibrant colored wings were painted vivid purples and greens. Haniah moved closer to get a better look. It was a girl with green hair and antennae on her head, like an insect. Its delicate facial features would have paired well with her mother's teacups. The creature flew behind another tree and Haniah followed it deeper into the forest.

"What are you?" Haniah asked, half to herself and half to the little pixie.

"I'm a fairy," she said with a giggle. She gestured with her finger for Haniah to follow. She spoke in a high pitch voice that barely disturbed the serenity of the surrounding trees. "What kind of animal are you?"

"I'm not an animal," said Haniah, tilting her head back to watch the fairy fly up into the leaves and back down again. "I'm a human."

"She's a human," repeated the fairy. From under a fern leaf, there came a second fairy, also giggling. This fairy had pink wings that shimmered in the thin streams of sunlight that broke through the branches above.

"Do you have any dreams?" asked the second fairy, fluttering about in front of her.

"Dreams?" asked Haniah, turning around to keep an eye on the fairies as they flew about. "I suppose so."

"Good. Come with us." The fairies giggled to one another and disappeared behind a thick tree that grew a hundred horses tall.

Haniah rounded the tree. There on the ground, plump mushrooms grew in a perfect circle. It was a peaceful sight, much like the silhouette of a full moon. Twenty or more fairies floated in the air above it. Stepping into the clearing, she spun, her dress pluming, to get a better look at them all. Some pink, some green, some blue. But all looked like shimmering butterflies.

She spun a second time and became lightheaded. She stilled herself, but the forest continued to spin. She dropped to the grass and the spinning slowed, but her vision became fuzzy. Haniah raised her hands to her head to calm the nausea. The fairies giggled. She saw glitter. No, gold. The color gold. Or was it gold coins? She couldn't quite make it out.

More glitter. She saw herself wearing a sparkling dress lined with diamonds and jewels. She grew very tired and thought she must be hallucinating. She could feel the weight of being pulled down into a dream.

More visions came of beautiful castles, colorful flags, and a royal crown.

The visions were all things she had dreamed of before, but now they came by force instead of invitation. She struggled to think about her family and why it was that she was traveling through the forest. Gradually, thoughts of her family were pulled from her mind, and all that was left was a blur. She had lost control of her thoughts, and now she closed her eyes. She lost herself to a dream. She let her body rest on the forest floor, her arm under her head. There she slept.

Somewhere in the darkness, there was a tug, a hook in her side that gently pulled. Quietly, it whispered her name, called to her. "Wake up." She could not make out the voice or where it came from, but something other than the visions had a hold on her.

When Haniah came to herself, she could not tell how long she had been out. "Barir," said Haniah, her vision clearing. She moved to the side of the Huggar and placed a hand on his back. Barir stirred and lifted his head. "Are you okay?"

"Yes. I'm okay."

"How did you find me?" she asked, looking toward the ring of mushrooms and then back to him.

"I came looking for you when I woke from my nap," he said as he sat up.

"You saved me!" She threw her arms around his neck. "I was lost in a dream."

"The Blue Gem saved us," said Barir, sitting on the ground. "After entering the circle of mushrooms my head began to spin, I began to have visions of my family and returning home. I then felt as if I was going to black out. I knew then I had to get the both of us out of the circle. I grabbed hold of Blue Gem just in time. It gave me enough strength to pull us both to safety."

"Yes, the gem saved us," Haniah said gratefully, glancing up.

The fairies above danced and laughed. They enjoyed the dreams and drama below.

"The Blue Gem?" asked a voice from behind them. "How interesting." The fairies that had been fluttering above flew into hiding at the sound of the voice. Behind trees and under ferns, they flew. Haniah turned to see a

JASON FORD

creature standing just outside of the grass-covered clearing. It was a man a little taller than she, but it wasn't a man. He had large pointed ears that rose above the highest part of his head. He wore a green tunic and brown leggings. He stood so still and blended into his surroundings so well, that she would not have seen him if he hadn't said something. "It appears you walked yourselves into a fairy circle."

"A fairy circle?" repeated Haniah.

"Yes," he said. "An enchanted fairy circle. I would also have tried to save you, but if I had, I too would be trapped and in danger of an eternal slumber. The fairies find great joy in the dreams of those they capture."

"The fairies," said Barir. "Where did they go?"

"They flew off," said the newcomer. "Let's just say their kind don't get along too well with my own." He took a step closer to inspect them and the circle of mushrooms. "I find it quite remarkable."

"What do you find remarkable?" asked Haniah, trying to assert some control over the situation.

"The enchantment of the fairies should be such that neither of you should be speaking to me right now. You should not have been able to escape." He placed his finger to his chin in thought. "Without this gem you speak of, I believe you would have been stuck here in an eternal sleep. It must be a very special gem." He looked at the backpack Barir carried.

"Who are you?" asked Haniah, getting to her feet. Having a stranger talk so freely about the gem made her defensive.

"I am Ghali." He raised the front of his hat in a polite gesture.

"Well, Ghali," said Barir, now towering over the pointy-eared crea-ture. "We have some place to be. If you don't mind, we will be moving on." He and Haniah picked up their packs and placed them on their backs. Haniah's sword was strapped to the pack. They gently brushed by and headed toward the trail they had been on. The stranger left the clearing and followed behind. Once on the trail, they headed south. The follower also turned south. Barir looked over his shoulder and saw Ghali walking among the trees. "Are you following us?" he asked.

"No. I am just out for a walk." He stepped over fallen logs and through tall ferns.

Barir and Haniah quickened their steps and the stranger matched their pace.

"I am not sure what this Elver is up to," he said, bending down to Haniah with his hand over his mouth in an attempt to let only her hear. "It is obvious he wished for us to see him. Otherwise he would not have let his presence be known. Elvers are very stealthy."

"That's an Elver?" Haniah whispered, looking at Ghali as he walked parallel to them.

"We also have keen hearing. No need to whisper," said Ghali. He gave a smile and another polite tip of his hat to Haniah. She turned her gaze away from him and faced the trail. "It would be wise to have a guide like myself. There are dangers in this forest."

Barir ignored the comment and turned from the path in the direction opposite the Elver. Ghali changed directions and followed behind Haniah.

"You are following us," Barir said as he looked over his shoulder and marched through the underbrush.

"I am not," countered Ghali. "Coincidentally, I'm just going in the same general direction as the two of you."

"That's following us." Barir changed his direction again.

"I wish you would not do that," said Haniah to the Elver behind her, frustration in her voice.

"Do what?" he asked innocently.

"Follow us!" said Haniah.

"Oh. Ok," said the green clad annoyance as he turned and walked the other direction. Haniah watched him go into the woods.

"I think he's gone," said Haniah.

"Good, last thing we need is a pesky Elver bugging us," said Barir.

Barir and Haniah continued walking, leaving the Elver out of sight. A short time later, they heard a tune being whistled beside them. They looked to their left to see the Elver walking next to them.

"Ugh!" Haniah sighed and placed her hands over her face in frustration.

"Where are you going?" asked the Elver in a pleasant tone.

"Searching for a tower," said Haniah.

"Not doing so well are you?"

"We are doing fine," Barir said. Though truthfully, he knew they had no idea where they were going.

"Could have fooled me," said the Elver as he gracefully moved to walk in front of them. "For the past two days you have crashed through these woods louder than a wailing ground moose. And you've been going in circles." Neither of them commented, knowing he was probably right. "Could it be the tower of Shahirah you're looking for?"

"Maybe," said Barir. "We don't have a name for it, but something very valuable is there."

"I know where it is." Ghali began to skip with excitement, but was careful not to lead too far ahead of them. "I can take you to it."

"How do you know it's the tower we seek?" asked Barir.

"For starters, there is only one tower in these woods. Second, it has a guard I have yet to get past, which leads me to think that whatever he is guarding is very valuable." His ears lifted when he smiled. They did not smile back. Ghali stopped in front of them and folded his arms. They stopped. "Do you or don't you want me to take you to it?"

"Would you?" asked Haniah with eagerness, showing her emotion. She did not know how she and Barir were ever going to find the place on their own.

"For a price."

"What price?" asked Barir.

"I need something." Without rustling a leaf, he walked around them.

"What is it you need?" asked Barir, bracing himself for a price they could not pay. All his money had been stolen.

"I need my bow back," said the Elver, speaking delicately and scratching behind his ear. "It's been taken from me."

"By whom?" asked Haniah.

"By the Ledians," he said.

"What's a Ledian?" asked Haniah.

"They are our first danger together," he said, grinning from ear to perky ear.

CHAPTER 11

Spirit Bow

Can you tell us more about these Ledians?" requested Haniah. "They are a group of Elver who live here in the forest, along the border of the West and East Kingdoms," said Ghali as he led them back to the trail.

"Why do they live there and not in the East with the other Elvers?" asked Barir.

"They are a sect who separated from the other Elvers three hundred summers ago," said Ghali. "It was after the Dark War and during the time when the Elvers and Humans agreed to live in peace with one another. The Ledians did not approve of the Human and Elver friendship. They chose to hold on to their old ways of thinking that all humans are bad and separated themselves from the other Elver. They are not friendly to outsiders. Especially human ones." He looked back at Haniah pointedly. "They think your kind an inferior race."

"They don't like humans?" Haniah could feel a lump form in her throat, realizing that he was taking her somewhere that others would be, at best, inhospitable to her.

"But don't take it personally," he said. "They don't like anyone. Not even their own race. They believe that Elvers are the one true race, but they think they are the chosen sect of the chosen race."

"They think they are better than everyone else?" asked Barir.

"Yes, something like that," said Ghali, taking a small game trail that would hardly have been noticeable if Haniah and Barir had been traveling alone. "They believe the Creator favors them above all others because of their rituals and practices. I think they are a little too arrogant if you ask me." He wrinkled his nose. "But you will just have to see for yourselves." He looked back at them. "You both look hungry." He pulled out a pouch from under his belt and handed it back to Barir who opened it to reveal two pieces of quiche. "Made it myself this morning." Barir handed one to Haniah and took a bite of the other.

"Thank you," said Barir.

"Yes, thank you," said Haniah. "I was getting so tired of eating plants."

"No problem," replied Ghali. "You will need your strength where we are going."

"How exactly can we help you?" asked Barir.

"These Ledians make a habit of claiming things for themselves," he said. "One of the things they have claimed as their own is actually mine."

"What kinds of things?" asked Barir.

"Treasures and artifacts mostly. They have my bow. We will need to make a trade for it. It's a magic bow, infused with spirit arrows."

"What's a spirit arrow?" asked Haniah, still enjoying the flavor of eggs. It was a welcome change from all the foliage she had been eating the past couple of weeks.

"Most arrows are made of wood, a material that is unlikely to do any real damage against steel or other metals. My bow is magical. Its arrows are able to pierce through any armor." He led them past moss-covered boulders, over several streams, and through a small meadow basked in sunlight before entering the trees again.

"Don't look around, but they are nearly here," said Ghali.

"Who?" asked Barir.

"The Ledians."

"How can you tell?" asked Haniah.

"I just know," he said, lowering his voice. "I would recommend that you do not reveal what you have in your satchels."

"You mean the gems?" asked Haniah, looking down at the pouch strung around her shoulder. She placed a hand over it. She looked at Barir, who gave her a concerned look.

"Yes," said Ghali. "Those are artifacts they would be most interested in having." He raised his hand for them to stop. Haniah nervously heeded his order. "It will be just a moment."

Barir and Haniah booth stood still for a moment, wondering what they were waiting for. Ghali did not move. The forest here was different. It was thick with vines and heavy leaves. They looked up at the branches of the tall, twisting trees above them. That's when they saw them.

They were dressed like Ghali, in greens and browns. They stood on tree limbs and among the leaves. There were a half dozen, all with bows drawn, pointed in their direction. One jumped from limb to limb until he reached the ground in front of them. He stood still, with an unmistakably unhappy face. He had dark eyes and a ring through his eyebrow. Haniah assumed he must be the one in charge.

"Search their satchels and take the Huggar's pack," said the Elver with the eyebrow ring. A second and third Elver jumped down from the trees and moved to take Haniah and Barir's belongings. Haniah held tightly to the satchel containing the gem. Barir placed a hand on his in an attempt to protect the gem hidden within.

"Stop," said Ghali. "These travelers are my guests, and under Elver law are not subject to search without my consent." The two Elvers paused and looked to their leader. He gave a quick nod of his head and the two

Elvers backed away.

"You will come with me." The Elver addressed them all without looking at one of them. He said no more and turned to walk through the woods.

Ghali followed the unhappy Elver and looked behind to see Barir and Haniah, still standing where he had left them. "Well, come along." He gestured with his hand for them to follow. Haniah loosened her grip on her satchel.

The tips of the arrows pointed in the direction Ghali, Haniah, and Barir walked as they fell into step behind the brooding Elver. The remaining Elvers took their place following the travelers down a dirt path.

They kept a brisk pace and marched single file through the woods. The path wove around fallen logs, through fern-filled meadows and over bubbling brooks.

"How is your day going?" Barir asked over his shoulder to the Elver who pointed an arrow at his back. The Elver frowned.

"You will speak when spoken to," said the guard, nudging Barir's back with a pointed elbow. "Keep walking."

The party of travelers walked under a canopy of leaves held high above their heads by towering trees. They were straighter and stronger than any trees Haniah had seen and the further into them they walked, the more she realized they had entered a dwelling or structure of some type. A living structure. A towering door opened up in their path, flanked to the side by a row of Elver guards. They passed the guards and entered into a splendid cathedral. The ceiling above was supported by giant trunks. The trees were pillars set to the side of an enormous ornate room. A crimson rug ran the length of the hall from where they entered to a dais at the other end. A beautiful, stained glass window provided vibrant color that filled the room. Upon the dais and directly below the glass window sat two Elvers, prominently placed on gold thrones. The female, who wore a crown of diamonds, had a face carved like unblemished marble. There was a male who wore a diamond ring on his right hand and an expression of cold, hard calmness like his companion.

A hushed reverence settled on Haniah as she noticed the grandeur of her environment and realized she was in the presence of royalty. Not pretend royalty, like in her books, but a real king and queen.

The company stopped just inside the throne room. The doors closed behind them with a thud. The brooding Elver guard who led them bowed to the ground and placed his knee to the floor and his fist on the plush rug.

Silence came from those who were already in the room. A small congregation of court orderlies mingled between the trees. All eyes lowered upon the entering of the guard.

The King let the stillness hang in the air before speaking. "You show your loyalty, faithful servant. You may rise." The guard stood again to face the King. He did not make any gesture or unneeded movement.

"With all reverence, I speak to your majesty," said the guard.

"Speak," commanded the regal figure.

"I present to you a wanderer we found walking through our woods." The guard stepped aside to reveal Haniah, Barir, and Ghali. The King's eyes passed over Haniah and Barir without any glimpse of recognition, but lingered on Ghali. There they stayed, burning holes into the Elver.

"You're back," said the King. "Are you here to account for your erroneous ways?"

"My only error was thinking for myself," Ghali said with defiance in his voice.

Haniah felt as though the air had been sucked from the room. Any serenity that might have existed in the chamber was there no longer, and she was left wondering who this Elver was to talk so disrespectfully to one as esteemed as a king.

Ghali's words seemed to have no effect on the stern figure. "Then what has brought you, if not humility?" asked the King, without a single hint of annoyance.

"I was just passing through the forest and thought I would stop to say hi," he responded. "Maybe get a bite to eat." He smiled a grin that showed white teeth.

"Please be serious." Not even an eyebrow was raised. "You never took things seriously."

"I have brought these two to meet you." With a grand wave of his arm, Ghali presented Haniah and Barir as if they were a framed piece of art. "I introduce them officially to Your Majesty now."

As if the visitors had only now been noticed, a gasp came almost simultaneously from everyone in the room.

"And why would you bring defilers into our sanctuary?" The volume in the King's voice rose with his last word. "Have you come to mock us?"

"I do not mock," said Ghali, with all sincerity. "I found these two in the forest. They escaped a fairy circle."

With this declaration, a stunned murmur filled the room. Disbelieving bystanders whispered to one another with hands over their mouths and lips pressed close to their neighbors' ear.

"You lie!" cried the King. "What you say is impossible."

"What I say is the truth."

The King's placid expression changed to rage. The Queen placed her hand on the King's arm to calm his nerves. They looked at one another and then back to Ghali. "The Queen and I shall confer on the matter and then determine what we shall do with you."

Seeing that the King and Queen were busy in quiet conversation, Haniah took the opportunity to step close to Ghali and whisper, "You're one of them, aren't you?"

"Yes," he spoke, leaning into Haniah so she could hear. "I used to live here, before I stopped believing everything they would have me believe."

"What are you saying?" demanded the King, now turning his attention to Ghali. "Speak up so we can all hear."

"I was just sharing with her that I too am a Ledian Elver," he responded. "I also said that we do not see things eye to eye." He spoke louder so all could hear. "I have been out and have met humans. I do not find them to be as objectionable as we make them out to be."

A second gasp sprang from the observers.

"They have polluted your mind," said the King, standing from his throne. "From your birth you were one of the chosen, and as such, were forbidden to mingle with the unclean race."

"That's just it. They aren't unclean." Ghali spoke with his hands open, arms at his side. "They are just like us." He could see the disgust begin to form on the King's brow.

"Our arms are always open," said the Queen softly and with earnest care in her voice. "You are always welcome with us. Please, reconsider what you have done, turn from these people, and return to us. Cast them off like the disease they are." Haniah could sense an urgent longing in her voice.

"I am always welcome with you so long as I believe like you." Ghali paused before continuing. "When are you going to understand that not everyone has to believe the same things to be one of the chosen?"

"Do not attempt to question your mother," bellowed the King with thunder in his voice. "You are walking on delicate ground. For millennia we have stood apart from all other races. It is our right and duty to keep clean from all that would soil our royal blood. We have been over this, son." The King stood and reached out his hand, pointing the finger with the diamond ring.

"Those are your parents?" asked Haniah under her breath.

"Yep," said Ghali.

"Ghali, Prince of the Ledian Elvers. I give you one last offer. Repent of your ways and come unto us." The King's voice was stern and uninviting. "What say you?"

"I cannot," said Ghali, taking a deep breath before continuing, "For I have not done anything wrong. I accept these people for who they are."

The Queen's expression turned to disappointment and the King's hardened. "So shall it be. You are hereby stripped of your royal title. Your name shall be blotted from the book of living life and upon your death, you shall not attain the height of a star. Your death will be one of Elven spirit. It is a spirit death you are granted."

A hushed murmur fell upon the audience. A young Elver girl ran out from around the pillar she had been watching from. "Ghali!" she called as she threw her arms around his waist and turned to the King. "Father! You can't do this. Please don't. Look at these people." She gestured to Haniah and Barir. "I believe Ghali. I don't think they are as evil as we have been made to believe."

"Samarah," said the King. "Move away from him. It must be done."

She tightened her grip on Ghali and he tightened his on her as they faced the King and Queen.

"Don't you see the harm you have done?" asked the Queen. "Your ideas influence even your sister. Your father's actions are an act of love. Now be gone!" She motioned with a wave of her hand.

Two Elver guards stepped forth, prepared to separate Ghali from his sister.

"It's ok, Samarah." He knelt down to look her in the eye. He placed his hands on her shoulders as he spoke. "I knew this day would come. I have been expecting it. What I was not expecting was how hard it would be." He watched as tears formed in her eyes and ran down her cheeks. "Please know, that though I will have to leave, I will always carry a piece of you with me." She reached out and wrapped her arms around his neck and squeezed.

"I love you," came a muffled cry.

"I love you, too." He pulled her away and placed a finger under her chin to lift her gaze. He smiled at her and wiped the tears from her cheeks. She stopped crying and smiled back. Ghali stood and motioned for his sister to move to the side and turned his attention once again to his parents.

"I will go but I seek one thing before I do," he said.

"What do you seek?" asked the King. "Speak carefully. You're no longer one of us. Your words will mark the path you take, your freedom or your death." Haniah could read the severity of the words in his face.

"I wish to have my bow back."

"Why would we do that?" The King would have laughed if not for his sternness. "We have no incentive to give it to you."

"Maybe you do."

"What do you have that would interest us in giving you something as powerful as the bow?"

"The girl," he said, tilting his head in the direction of Haniah. He continued with a wry smile. "She will make a great servant, or a sacrifice, if you wish."

Haniah stumbled back in shock at hearing Ghali's proposition. No one in the room smiled.

"You can have her. Indoctrinate her and send her back out into the world with a better understanding of her uncleanliness." This comment struck closer to the Elver way of thinking. The King took a moment to rub his chin in consideration.

"You tricked us!" Haniah charged at Ghali with raised fists.

The guard stepped between Haniah and Ghali and grabbed Haniah by the arm. "There will be no disruptions while in His Majesty's presence."

"You dirty…You rotten…" Haniah exclaimed while still attempting to get at Ghali. Her tongue searched for the most vile words she could think of to express her disgust. "You brought us here to trade us for your bow. You pig!"

Ghali did not seem to give any more notice to Haniah as she struggled with the guard. He waited quietly for the King's response.

"Make it noted," said the King, gesturing to an Elver who stood to the side of the dais. He wore an ornately decorated cape and held parchment and a pen. "We accept the exchange. The girl will be traded for the Spirit Bow. Ghali will then, at once, leave and never return." The scribe wrote as the King continued, "She will be taken to the lower chambers and be there imprisoned for thirteen summers."

"Thirteen summers!" exclaimed Ghali. "That's a little long, don't you think?"

"You are no longer one of us, deserter." The words were a dagger, hurled through the air at his son. Ghali's face winced in pain. "You can no longer make that judgment."

"Father, I am not a deserter. We just see things differently."

"Your mother and I lived through the Dark War three hundred summers ago. We know the pain these people have caused. The humans are evil. Even now, word comes from our scouts that they are as bad as ever, their greed for money consumes them. They are willing to stab one another in the back and are still not able to forgive each other. We will make the trade for no other reason than to save her from their heretic ways. Trust me, we would not wish her here if we could have it any other way. We will teach her the true order of things and then release her when we see fit."

The Queen tugged on the King's cloak and he leaned in to hear her whisper. They both turned their attention to Barir. "Huggar, we have words for you. You may go your way. Our people have lived in relative peace for many seasons, and we do not wish to upset our current course. But, know that you travel with a deserter. If you continue to travel with him, he will also desert you. He will desert you in your time of need. He has deserted us and his ways just as he has deserted this young human. He will desert you. That is what he does."

"We did have an arrangement, but it would appear that the arrangement has changed." Barir bent his waist in an attempt to show as much respect as he could. "I will take your words as an advisement."

Haniah looked at Barir, realizing there was nothing he could do. She turned and glared at Ghali. He lowered his head toward his toes.

"Go get the bow!" the King declared.

A guard standing near a pillar jumped into motion with the King's words and returned shortly with the glistening white bow. To Haniah, it looked as though it were carved from some kind of marble, but it was handled delicately and seemed to be much too light to be stone. She then thought it might be made from the bone of a large animal, but the bow was far more glossy and smooth than any bone could be polished. There were intricate swirls carved into the bow that flowed with its curves and gave the appearance of crashing waves. No worked piece of wood she had ever seen showed such craftsmanship and beauty. The guard approached Ghali and handed him the bow.

"Now that is taken care of," continued the King, "take the girl to the prison."

"You can't do this!" Haniah protested as a second guard came and grabbed her free arm. He and the guard with the eyebrow ring moved her toward an exit at the side of the room. Haniah twisted and turned to get away, but the Elvers had firm grips. Her heels drug across the ground. She realized that struggling was hopeless and that she would not get away using her strength. Her mind raced, searching for a way out of her situation.

"Wait! I can make you a better deal!" said Barir.

"Speak." The King raised an open palm and the guards holding Haniah stopped where they were.

"May I please counsel with my companion?" he gestured to Haniah.

"You may, quickly," said the King.

Barir moved to where Haniah was being held. He whispered into her ear as the Elvers in the room looked on. Barir gave a nod with his large head and they separated.

"What if I could provide you with the hidden locations of the Gems of Anwar?" asked Barir. "Would that be enough to set her free?"

"Is what you say true, Huggar?" asked the King.

"It is true, Your Majesty. We have a way of knowing where the gems are hidden."

"Then I will make the trade, and she shall be set free," said the King, now speaking to Haniah.

Haniah moved her eyes from one guard to the other and back to the King. The King lifted a finger, and they loosened their grip. With a jerk, she pulled her arms free from their grasp and walked over to Barir. He bent down to let her into his pack. She reached in and pulled out a thick, red, bound book.

"In this book are prophecies containing clues to the locations and natures of the gems." She held the book out in front of her. The King's eyes widened. One of the guards that had been holding her walked up to her. She handed him the book, and he carried it to the King. The King carefully turned the pages with his fingers before closing it, satisfied.

"You are free to go," said the King, speaking to both Haniah and Barir. "With some stipulations. You are never to return and are to remember our words. Ghali is a deserter and will desert you in your time of need." The King turned and took his seat once again.

The large doors opened behind them and they turned to leave. With his bow, Ghali followed Barir, and Barir followed Haniah out into the forest.

CHAPTER 12

The Tower and a Lesson

"Not all Elver are like my parents," said Ghali. He followed Haniah as they walked. They had been walking for almost an entire day. The guards had escorted them far from where they had met the King and Queen and then turned back. "I just want you to know that."

"I'm hoping they're not all like *you*," she retorted. "I have to say, I am not impressed with what happened back there." She stopped and turned on him, poking him in the chest with a pointed finger. "Not only with your parents, but with you." Her anger was apparent in her furrowed brow.

"I wouldn't have left you there," he said, leaning back on his heels. "I just didn't have anything else to trade with them. You were the best thing I had to offer."

"I was bait to bring out the bow?"

"Yes."

"I could have been sacrificed!"

"They don't sacrifice people. That was a joke." He grinned widely. "Funny, don't you think?"

"I am not laughing." She raised her finger as if threatening to poke him again.

"If I didn't offer you, they never would have brought out my bow. Once I had my bow, I could have fought our way out of there."

"It is much better that it turned out the way that it did," she said. "My friend, Mr. Barir here, doesn't like to fight."

"Look at him," said Ghali, sizing Barir up with his eyes. "He doesn't fight?"

"No, he doesn't." There was a hint of annoyance in her voice.

"Could have fooled me," said Ghali, still interested in talking about Barir's unusual size. "If I had arms like him, I'd be the greatest fighter in all the land."

Barir gave a shrug to show his lack of interest in the Elver's line of thinking.

"I am not sure if I am going to like you or not, Mr. Ghali." She turned to march down the trail. "Barir, what do you think of those Elver we met today?"

"They are the most peculiar Elver I have come across. It is true what Ghali has said, not all Elver are like those ones. Not all Elver have such radical views."

"I did not like them," Haniah said.

"Do not dislike them." He spoke deliberately. "Feel for them or even pity them, but do not dislike them. Dislike only cankers your heart. People like them are fearful."

"Fearful of what?"

"They fear that what they believe just might not be true. That is why they make the dire declarations they do."

"Like 'all humans are evil'?"

"Yes," he confirmed. "Like, 'all humans are evil.' Or that they are the only 'chosen people.' The sad part is that they don't even know they are scared. So feel for them, but do not dislike them."

They came to a brook running over a small cascade of rocks. Haniah stooped down and took a drink. "This will make a good place to stop for the night, don't you think, Barir?" The sun had sunk behind the trees, painting the sky orange and leaving shadows across the land.

"Yes, I think here will be just fine." he said as he took off his backpack and placed it close to himself. "I do have a concern, Haniah."

"What is it?" she asked. Ghali took a seat on a log and stopped to listen.

"Without my book of prophecies, how are we going to find the remaining gems?"

"We already have two of them, the white and the blue. The King and Queen don't know that, and we have a head start on locating the Green Gem. That leaves finding the location of the Red Gem. I believe the location of the Red Gem is on my father's map. That we still have."

"That we do," said Barir positively.

Haniah moved away from the spring and walked over to face Ghali. "Now for you to stick to your end of the deal."

He grinned sheepishly.

"How much further until we reach the tower?" she asked.

"About a two day walk. South, through the woods."

"Then we will continue our journey at first light in the morning," said Barir, patting down an area of tall grass. "I am tired. I'm going to turn in for the night." He placed his head on his pack. He rolled to his side and closed his eyes.

"You're royalty?" She lowered her voice so as not to disturb Barir and his attempt at sleep.

"I used to be." Ghali patted a place on the log next to him as a gesture for her to sit.

"What was it like?" she asked, taking the spot next to him.

Ghali was silent for a moment as he pondered the question. "Like anything else, I guess." He shrugged his shoulders. "Being royalty doesn't shield you from pain or sorrow." The hurt he was feeling from being treated so poorly by his parents sat close to the surface. "I will miss my family, but I don't miss being a prince. I am still the same person I was yesterday." Having dreamed of being royalty, Haniah listened attentively as Ghali continued. "I find the world to be so much bigger than the way my parents see it, and the way I used to see it. Other races have so much to offer. I think there is so much beauty in the world, in its diversity and differences. I would give up being a prince for these realizations any day. I started seeing the differences in the people who would pass through our woods on occasion. When I first left my parents, I lived in the woods. I seldom approached travelers who wandered through the woods, and they never seemed to notice me. I watched them from afar. For forty summers, I watched them and have realized that they are more like me than I once thought. But even with this knowledge, I was always afraid to venture out of the forest."

"Forty summers?" asked Haniah with surprise. To her, he looked to be about twenty. "That's a long time. How old are you?"

"I am two hundred and six summers old," he said proudly.

"Do you feel old?"

"No, not at all. I am still young. It takes many more seasons for an Elver to become an adult than it does for your people."

"When you left the Elver, why did you not leave the forest?" asked Haniah.

"I was a little scared of what I might find." Ghali's mouth hinted at a frown. "What if the world turned out to be like what I was taught when I was younger? Full of hateful humans and dangerous ways. Or worse, what if there was something wrong with me, and the world didn't like me? It just felt safer in the woods. And now I'm glad that I stayed as long as I have. If I had not been in the woods today, I might not have met you and Barir." He gave her his wry smile.

"This part of the world is willing to give you a chance. I am betting on you to be a good person." She looked him in the eye. "After all, if you really had it in for us, you would have tried trading the gems we carry. You did not do that. For that, I will give you a little trust."

"Thank you." A hint of a tear formed in the corner of his eye. "Sometimes I make mistakes, but I mean no harm." He wiped his eyes dry. "I guess, like everyone else, I just want to be accepted."

"You should get some sleep," Haniah said.

"Yes, I am tired." He moved close to where Barir slept and began to make the tall grass a bed. "You should go to sleep as well."

"I will."

Ghali laid down, closed his eyes, and fell asleep. In the quiet of the night, Haniah pulled her silver locket from around her neck. She had kept the necklace and the gem hidden from the Elver, but now with Ghali sleeping she felt comfortable using it. It cast a little glowing light on her face as she opened it. There, in the glass, was a picture of Ghali. Two little green arrows sat on its edge, one pointing to where Barir slept and the other to where Ghali lay in the grass. Haniah closed the magic necklace with a sense of assurance that, for now, she was safe.

The sky had turned dark. Haniah sat on the log and pondered her situation. Never would she have imagined that someday she would be so far from home and in the company of an Elver and Huggar. Only in her wildest dreams had goblins and dragons existed. She would have been astonished if she had been told that she would see a real king and queen. In light of all these adventures and experiences, she felt alone. She looked up to the sky, searching…searching. Faintly she could see them. Three specks of light twinkled far away. She could see the stars that refused to go out. They shined like a beacon as if with a message, *Press on and keep going.*

❧❧

The company stood before a wall of tangled thorns. They had traveled two days without incident and had arrived at the desired location. They could see the top of a tower poking out from behind the thorny wall.

"Now how are we going to get past this?" asked Barir after they had walked the entire circumference of the wall, looking for any crack in its fortification. Once, Haniah had tried to squeeze through what looked like a hopeful opening, only to have the twisting thorns close in on her and force her to move back.

"It's almost as if they have a mind of their own," said Ghali, shifting his weight on his feet.

"If we try going through them we will get shredded," said Barir, scratching his head.

Haniah pulled out the sword she had been carrying at her waist and walked in between Ghali and Barir, who were both still looking at the wall. She took a swing. Barir dodged the sword and Ghali ducked. *Thwapsh!* Hard and swift she cut through the first branch. *Thwoosh!* A second swing dug deeper into the tangled mass of thorns and dropped them to the ground. Other thorns moved in to fill the gap. Haniah swung again to drop the newcomers and moved forward. She swung again, and again. Faster than before, so as not to let newer thorns fill the void she had just created. "Follow me!" she yelled, still swinging.

She was a storm of motion and chaos. Always moving forward, never looking back. Debris from the thorn wall flew in every direction. A thorn the length of her hand caught her shoulder and caused her to bleed. Still she swung. The others followed until they reached the other side of the barrier and out into a grassy meadow. Haniah fell, panting. Exhausted, she laid down, catching her breath. Barir and Ghali stood on a green field dotted with little purple flowers.

"Wow!" said Barir, coming over to help Haniah up. "I didn't know you had that in you."

She brushed herself off, and together they gazed up at a single spire. Even Barir had to bend his neck back to see the top of it.

"The Tower of Shahirah." Ghali stood with his hands on his hips. "Legend has it that fifty thousand have died trying to enter its walls. The only ones to return after being inside have come back out of their mind. It is said to be cursed with dark magic." At this, Haniah and Barir froze where they stood.

"Let's not just stand here." Ghali walked up to a wood door at the base of the tower.

"Maybe we should rethink this before we go in there," said Barir.

"Are you going to believe everything you hear?" asked Ghali, not giving a hoot about what he had just said. The Elver placed a hand on the door. Haniah and Barir shared a frightened look and then followed.

The door opened, and they walked into a large circular room made of stacked stone blocks, each about the size of a man. The air smelled musty, and the dust-covered floor showed that no living thing had crossed the room for many seasons. The corners where the floor met the wall were dark. In the middle of the open space was an erect figure, standing still. A green translucent glow around the individual gave light to the room.

"I knew you would come," spoke the glowing figure. Oddly, the three travelers could see the back wall through his body. He wore a polished breast plate and helmet. Haniah was troubled by the sword at his side and the shield on his arm. She raised her sword.

"Come to fight I see," said the figure.

"We have come for the Green Gem," said Haniah.

"I see. Then we shall have a duel. If you win, I will give you the gem."

"A duel to the death?" asked Barir.

"No, no." The man chuckled. "Not a duel to the death. We cannot have a duel to the death when I am already dead."

"You're a ghost then," Ghali surmised.

"Yes I am." His fingers twisted a long mustache. "I am the Ghost Knight Sir Amid, guardian of the Green Gem. I was placed here by a personal request from the late Queen Anwar herself." He pulled from his sheath a glistening sword. "Be proven worthy of the gem or leave without it. Now which one of you shall duel first?"

"I will," said Haniah, stepping forward with her sword pointed at the knight.

"Well, don't hesitate then. Come after me."

Haniah raised her sword above her head and lunged forward, missing the knight as he stepped to the side.

"Not bad, but you will have to do better than that. Keep your chin up when you charge and always look where you are going."

Haniah lunged again, keeping her eyes on the ghost knight as she did. He stepped to the side again and Haniah swung her sword in the direction he moved. He blocked her swing with the tip of his sword.

"Very good. Much better. You see, I had to defend your move that time."

The man had a spring in his step in spite of being old and, of course, a ghost. Haniah thought he had probably seen seventy summers. Maybe more. But he moved with grace, a butterfly dancing in a breeze. With every move she made, he countered it with little effort and then gave her advice as though he were helping a friend. "Keep your feet apart. Balance the blade in your hand. Think two moves ahead," he would say. Haniah swung, lunged, and dived, trying to keep up with the Knight's instruction.

"I saw how you barged your way through the thorns. You used brute strength. You will need to use some finesse to beat me."

"We will see about that!" cried Haniah in mid charge. Her sword came cracking down on Sir Amid's raised shield. Swing after swing she gave all her strength to beating him. Unlike the thorns that gave way to her repeated strikes, the shield did not yield, and blow after blow her strength drained.

With a swift slice the knight countered with a swing that sent Haniah's sword spiraling out of her hand and onto the cold floor some distance from her.

"You must learn to keep a tighter grip." He pointed his sword at her, commanding her to stay where she was. "Never let go of your sword in defeat. Hold on to it. Only let go when you have chosen to. You should not let anyone else make that decision for you, whether you're beaten or not, whether you're exhausted or out of fight. Do not let go." He spoke so passionately that his mustache quivered with every syllable. "When you let go, it should be your decision, and your decision alone." When he finished speaking, he lowered his sword.

"You were toying with me," said Haniah angrily. "Why not give me your best? I can take it."

"I was not toying with you," said Sir Amid. "I was teaching you. You fight with tenacity and emotion. You're a quick learner—with a little practice you will be a great swordsman. You may even save someone's life some day with your skills. But today they have not proven you worthy of the Green Gem." He turned his attention to Barir, and Haniah walked over to pick up her sword. "Do you wish to challenge me for the gem, Huggar?"

"I do not fight," he said, taking a bow and stepping back.

"How about you Elver?" Sir Amid pointed his gloved hand at Ghali. "Do you wish to fight?"

"I don't have a sword. I have a bow. It is designed to fight evil and will penetrate any thickness of armor, but I don't know if it would have any effect upon the likes of you."

"Are you a Seeker?"

"Yes, I am. I guess," said Ghali.

"Then why don't you just try asking me if you may have the gem?" The ghost knight rested his hands on the hilt of his sword.

He looked to Haniah and Barir with a puzzled look before responding. "May I have the gem?" he asked, thinking it was some kind of trick.

"Maybe. Try saying it with a 'please'."

"Please, may I have the gem?" he asked flatly and with a smirk.

"Yes," replied Sir Amid. He gave a large grin, and his mustache turned up around his cheeks.

"What?" asked Haniah incredulously. "All we had to do was ask you for it?"

"Well, yes," said the knight. "You would be surprised how many come here wanting to fight. And they always forget to use their manners."

Haniah's mouth dropped open, and the three of them stood staring at Sir Amid in astonishment.

"Ok, so where is it?" asked Ghali.

"It is above you."

Ghali tilted his head back to look up. Far above their heads at the top of the tower was a swirling, spiraling mist of flashing lights. "What is that?" he asked.

"It's a portal," said the knight. "Enter there and find the Green Gem."

"Aren't you going to get it for me?"

"No."

"No? But you just said you would give it to me." Ghali placed his hands on his hips.

"I will give it to you, but you must retrieve it." The knight pointed up to the portal.

Ghali looked around the room for a staircase or ladder with no luck. There was no apparent way to get up to it. "How am I supposed to get up there?"

Sir Amid's help consisted of a shrug and a slight tilt of his head.

Puzzled, Ghali walked to the wall of the tower in an attempt to climb it. He dug his fingers into the small crack between the stones, but his grip slipped when he placed weight on his hands, and he remained firmly planted to the ground.

"I have an idea," said Haniah. She tugged on Barir's sleeve. He bent down and she whispered into his ear.

"Come over here, Ghali," said Barir, setting down his backpack. He pulled from it the Blue Gem.

"What are you going to do?" asked Ghali.

"I am going to throw you," he said in his deep rumbling voice, giving Ghali a good-natured wink.

"Oh, that sounds safe," he said sarcastically.

"Just come over here." Barir motioned to him, and Ghali moved to stand next to Barir. "I'll throw you up to that ledge and you can grab it." High above them, and just below the turning portal was a skinny ledge.

Looking up at the ledge, Ghali's voice wavered as he spoke. "That's way too high for even you to throw me."

Without giving Ghali any more time to protest, Barir grabbed him by the arm. With his large hands, he was able to hold the gem and grab Ghali's feet. With one huge thrust upward, he sent the Elver flying through the air. Ghali reached out and grabbed the ledge. "I got it!" he said.

Placing his elbow up on the ledge, he pulled himself up to stand on it. He jumped up without delay and vanished into the portal.

Barir placed the Blue Gem back into his backpack and once again placed its straps over his shoulders.

"Now what do we do?" asked Haniah.

"I guess we wait," said Barir.

"Aaaahhhhh!" Ghali yelled as he fell through the air. He waved his arms and legs frantically. Barir reached his arms out just in time to keep Ghali from hitting the floor.

Ghali lay in Barir's arms. "Barir, it's you!" Ghali hugged Barir like he was a long-lost friend. "I didn't know if you would still be here when I got back." Ghali took Barir's face in his hands and began to cry with joy.

Barir pulled back and placed Ghali's feet gently on the ground. Ghali looked around him and, seeing Haniah, rushed over to her and picked her up in his arms. "Haniah, I am so glad to see you!"

"What has gotten into you?"

"After being gone for so long I didn't know if you would both still be here."

"What are you talking about?" asked Barir "You jumped into the portal only a moment ago."

"But I have been gone so long, and done so much." He looked exhausted and spoke honestly. He reached into a bag he had over his shoulder and pulled out a Green Gem that filled the palm of his hand.

"How did you get that?" asked Haniah.

"I cannot say. There is so much to tell and not enough time to tell it," he said, looking at Haniah. "We have to continue on our quest. The world is not safe until the Golden Gem is found, and we still have to find the Red." He then turned to Barir. "There are some things I wish to share with you, but cannot at this time." Barir raised his arms above his shoulders as Ghali hugged the Huggar around his thick waist. "I am just so glad to see you."

"You are now the guardian of the gem," said Sir Amid, stepping forward. "I am relinquished of my post. I thank you." After giving a bow of respect to Ghali, he continued. "I am free to join my ancestors in the stars. May they yet return." With his final words, the ghost knight's image slowly disintegrated, leaving behind the three friends and a darkened room.

Haniah, Barir, and Ghali all exited into the sunlight. Together, the three guardians set out from the tower, across the meadow, beyond the thorns and into the woods with a renewed commitment to finding the Golden Gem.

CHAPTER 13

Dark Hearts

THE DWARF LET OUT A RAGGED BREATH AS HE HUNG, CHAINED, IN A dark cavern. His wrists bled from the shackles that supported his weight. He had lost hope long ago, broken and exhausted. The cause of his pain was a wizard in an ebony robe with red lining, who was now moving across the room.

A witheram with red eyes and filed teeth accompanied him. It had pointed ears, purple-black skin and carried a serated knife at its side. Once a goblin, its body and soul had been disfigured by the evil magic of the wizard.

Together, they approached their prisoner from the other side of the chamber. The witheram looked on with gleeful excitement at the grief apparent on the prisoner's face. The creature bent close to the wizard and groveled to its master.

"Do it! Do it Master!" The witheram wrung its hands with anticipation.

"Don't crowd me!" screamed the wizard as he hit it in the head with a swing of his staff. The wretched creature fell to the cold floor. He stood back up, hunched over as it was.

To the dwarf on the wall, the wizard was darkness and despair in human form. Enchanting a spell, the wizard pointed a finger at the dwarf's chest. Stooping low but never actually touching the prisoner, he twisted his finger around and around in small circles. The motion burrowed deep into the dwarf's skin. The crystal on top of the wizard's staff glowed red. The witheram's eyes opened wide as he watched with enthusiasm, feeding off the prisoner's pain. Grinning, he licked his moist lips with his twisted tongue. The dwarf's heart began to wilt and turn cold and dark. Each twist of the wizard's finger drew out what faint remnants of good feeling the heart once held. Tenderness, kindness, and warmth were all lost and replaced by fear, terror, contempt and bitterness. The dwarf's shoulders caved, and his head dropped.

Intoxicated, the witheram cackled and rolled around on the floor on his hands and knees.

"Tell me, when did you see them last?" demanded the wizard.

"I have told you already." The dwarf let out a moan.

"Tell me again. I'd like to hear it again," said the evil wizard. It was the tremble in Hadi's voice he enjoyed the most.

"It was at the top of the mountain."

"How long ago?" He leaned in to hear the rasping of the prisoner's lungs.

"Three sunrises ago." The red glow of the staff reflected the beads of sweat that had formed on his face. "Maybe five." The wizard glared with uncaring eyes. Laboring, Hadi continued. "I don't really know."

"You say it was a Huggar and a girl. Where were they going?"

Hadi was too exhausted to speak. This had not been the first, nor even the second round of questioning that day. The wizard turned his finger again and Hadi felt the pain burn his insides.

"They sought passage to the stairs of Jabal," he said, gritting his teeth.

"Do you know what for?"

The dwarf shook his head slightly, his neck no longer able to support his head to face his oppressor.

"Are you afraid, little man?" Darkness leaned in and let the last two words linger on his lips.

Hadi let out a pathetic whimper. His body began to shake.

"I believe we are ready," he said, turning his back to the prisoner. He moved, cape flowing behind him, over to a large cauldron sitting in the middle of the room. He spoke an enchantment, waving the staff in front of him. The gem waxed hot and black smoke rose from the charred pot. A single gold coin, taken from the dwarf not long before, was pulled from a satchel and ceremoniously dropped into the cauldron. The coin began to bubble and smoke. A small hiss escaped from the mixture and a pillar of poisonous vapor rose like a funnel into the air, parting to reveal a specter standing above the cauldron.

The witheram cowered into a corner to avoid its gaze and hid in the shadows. Hadi, still hanging on the wall, closed his eyes in terror. Near death, his heart ached. The wizard opened his arms out wide, his cloak spreading like dark triumphant wings.

"Who summons the Specter Death?" The specter spoke faintly, as though its voice came from a different world.

"Your Lord and Master, Amjad Fatih, Conqueror of the Great, Prince and Wizard of Daybreak."

"Why am I summoned, my Lord?"

"You are summoned to do my bidding," said the wizard, voice riddled with sinister pleasure.

"What is thy bidding?" Vapor passed between its bone white teeth as it spoke.

"I seek a gem. It is believed to be in the possession of a girl and a Huggar," said the wizard, pleased with his power and the arrival of the nightmare before him. "A witheram was on their trail. They escaped in the North Mountains of Hayud. There were no trails left in the snow off of the mountain. They likely escaped using Huggar magic."

"Huggar magic is weak and easily thwarted," said the specter. "They will not have gotten far."

"That is as I hoped," said Darkness, turning to point at the prisoner. "This dwarf saw them last."

Knowing the fate of those he had stolen from, Hadi's pain consumed his soul. He had told them he would help them up the mountain. Guilt ran through his body. An audible cry broke from his lungs. The wizard turned his staff on the prisoner and enchanted a spell that struck Hadi silent. Hadi's heart was dead, his body too exhausted for tears.

"He provided us with these," said the wizard, holding out a satchel of coins. "They were stolen. The evilness of his act of theft left residue on them. You can use it to track the Huggar." Amjad Fatih flipped the satchel into the air. The specter's gloved fist snatched the satchel in flight.

"It shall be done."

"You are to find out what they know about finding the Golden Gem," said the wizard. "Your deceptive skills will be needed."

"Yes, Master."

"One more thing." The wizard paused, taking special pleasure in thinking about what he was going to say next. "Before you kill them, make sure they know they are about to die." He tapped a pointed finger on his grinning lips before waving his arm at the monster. "Now be gone."

Morphing into a cloud of smoke, Death flew out the door and down the hall of the hidden chamber.

Once the specter had left, the witheram came out of its hiding place. "What would you have me do with this one?" it asked, snapping its teeth at Hadi.

"Release him," said the wizard. He moved in the direction the specter had left. "He is under my power, and devious servants are always needed."

CHAPTER 14

Wolves

IT'S GOT TO BE CLOSE TO SUPPER TIME," said Haniah. Barir drank thirstily from his canteen. "I'm going to go look for some food."

The forest had thinned over the past few hours and they now walked through ground foliage and sparsely placed trees.

Ghali's stomach growled. "I'll come with you."

"I'm going to rest here." Barir sat down and leaned against his backpack.

"We will be back soon," said Ghali.

They wandered some distance as they picked berries and dug up roots. After a while, Haniah decided to take a rest on a rock.

"Wait! Don't sit there!" Ghali yelled with an outstretched hand.

Too late—the creature had reached around and grabbed Haniah, its solid arms holding her firm. She screamed, her legs kicking frantically in the air.

"Don't struggle! The more you struggle, the tighter they hug."

"Hug?" Haniah could barely speak. The air in her lungs was being pushed out of her.

Ghali stood, feet spread wide, arms outstretched, his balance low to the ground. All around him, the rocks in the area came to life.

"What is it?" Barir growled, crashing through the brush. He stopped abruptly when he noticed Ghali's frenzied wave.

"Be quiet," said Ghali in a hushed tone. "They don't have any eyes, but they can hear."

With outstretched arms, several jagged-edged rock creatures moved in the direction of Ghali's voice, looking for something to hug.

Barir looked at Haniah, whose face was beginning to turn blue. "We can't just stand here, it's killing her!" Barir stepped back as one of the rocks turned toward him.

"You have to tickle them," whispered Ghali, sneaking around the back of one of the rocks. He placed his hand in a crevice where its neck might be.

"Tickle them?"

"They have soft undersides." Ghali wiggled his fingers. A deep rumble came from inside the creature's chest as it tried to escape. Falling to the ground, the rock laughed a deep and hearty laugh.

Barir moved to the side of the rock squeezing Haniah. Placing his hands underneath the rock's arms he began to tickle. It laughed and laughed the more he wiggled his fingers. Releasing its hold, Haniah fell to the ground panting for air and holding her neck.

"I got these," said Ghali moving to the other rock creatures. The ones that had already been tickled curled back up into static form.

"Are you ok?" asked Barir, kneeling down at Haniah's side.

"I'm ok." She took a deep breath. "I'm just a little shaken."

Ghali came to stand next to them once the rest of the rocks had been taken care of.

"What were those?" asked Barir.

"Rock Hobblers," answered Ghali. "They can be found throughout the forest. There's no real danger if you know what to do."

"Well, I am glad you were with us," said Barir.

"Sometimes the hardest creatures just want a little attention, and the best way to give it is to tickle them." Ghali shared a triumphant smile.

Together they walked to get the backpack Barir had left behind when running to Haniah's aid. Sitting on the backpack was a small bird. It was a common brown bird with a little beak and yellow legs.

"Hello, little bird." Haniah held out a finger to the animal. Surprisingly, it jumped onto her finger.

"Look. It has something tied to its leg," said Barir.

Haniah untied a piece of tightly rolled paper from the bird's leg. It was about the size of her fingernail, but when she unwound it, she found that it stretched the length of her arm. "It's a message." The bird jumped back to its place on the backpack.

"What does it say?" asked Ghali.

Haniah read:

To whom this message is delivered,

I hope this salutation finds you well. I am, at the moment, indisposed. I wish for you to make haste out of Shahirah forest. A day's journey south of the forest, you will find a small cottage. I have sent a message informing the occupants of your arrival. You will know its location once you approach a small stream with two hills to either side. Look for the blue chimney smoke. Once there, you will find food, rest, and aid for your injuries.

With regards,

Nuwairah

First Wizardess of the Three Circles

"Who is it addressed to?" asked Ghali.

"It doesn't give a name." Haniah turned the paper over in her hands.

"Is the message for us?" asked Ghali.

"I don't know," Haniah said. She looked to Barir for an answer.

"We are in the Shahirah forest," he said. "The letter is addressed to a party in the Shahirah forest." He rubbed his chin with the back of his hand and looked to Ghali. "It could be us. I mean, how many parties could be in the forest right now?"

"In all my many summers in the forest, not very many parties have passed through. One or two a season at most." Ghali pointed to the signature on the note. "Who is this Wizardess of the Three Circles?"

"I have met her," said Haniah, turning to Barir. "She visited my family on the night of the attack."

"Is she someone we can trust?" asked the Elver.

"So far she has saved my life and given me hope for saving my family."

"Is it a letter we can trust?" asked Ghali. "Do we know it comes from who it says it is from?"

"You sure are thorough in your misgivings." Barir glanced at him out of the corner of his eye.

"That I am. I also find it odd that it says we will find aid for our injuries when none of us actually have any injuries." Ghali stretched out his arms to show he was injury free and looked over the healthy bodies of Haniah and Barir. He punctuated his comment with a doubtful smirk.

With that thought, Barir scratched the top of his head with a blunt finger. Back and forth, back and forth went his finger as he contemplated.

"What should we do, Barir?" asked Haniah.

"This is a puzzle. A puzzle I do not have an answer to. I would agree, none of us are injured. I would defer to your judgment, Haniah."

Haniah creased her brow in thought. "I would like to take a vote. I think we should all have a say in where we go and what we do."

"Very well. We will vote."

"Raise your hand if you think we should follow the letter and travel to the cottage between the two hills." Haniah raised her hand as she spoke. Barir looked down at her and also lifted his hand above his head. Both Haniah and Barir looked at Ghali, their hands still in the air. Slowly, Ghali raised his. "Ok, it's unanimous. Out of the woods we go." With that, the bird fluttered its wings, took to the air, and flew away.

"We picked some berries and dug up some roots," said Ghali, emptying the contents of his pockets on the ground. "We might as well have a bite to eat while we are stopped."

"Good idea." Barir took a seat and picked up the white root Ghali had presented.

Haniah pulled a bag of berries from her satchel and sat next to Barir.

"Do you have any family, Barir?" asked Ghali, taking a seat on the ground to complete the circle.

"I have a wife and a baby boy." Barir smiled at their memory. "I hope to get back to them soon. It's been hard being away from them as long as I have." He paused before adding, "But being with Haniah helps me carry on."

"How so?" asked Haniah.

"Seeing you gives me hope that my boy will grow up and be as courageous as you some day."

"I'm not brave," said Haniah, waving her hand to dismiss his remark.

"I think you are. And who knows, maybe someday you will come to know it for yourself," said Barir. "My wife is beautiful and kind." He gazed off into the distance, her memory bringing sweet feelings to his heart. "The first time I saw my baby boy, my joy was greater than I thought it could ever be. The rewards of being a father have surpassed anything else I have done in my life."

"Then why did you leave them?" asked Haniah.

"The state of the world compelled me to leave. Evil would have eventually spilled over into the North Kingdom, threatening their lives. I have to do what I can to stop that from happening."

Haniah reached into her satchel and pulled out her brother's wooden toy horse. Internally, Haniah thought about her brother Najid and regretted fighting with him the last time she had seen him.

"What is that?" asked Ghali, pointing to the toy.

"It's my brother's." The sorrow that came when she thought about her missing family showed in Haniah's eyes. "He and my parents were attacked by goblins and taken from me."

"Taken?" asked Ghali. "Where?"

"I am not sure where. But I am going to get them back." She spoke earnestly.

"They must be very special to you to search for them like you do," said Ghali.

"My father is kind and hard working," Haniah confided. "My mother was someone I could tell anything to, and my brother was sweet." Haniah turned her sight to the sky.

"What do you know of your ancestors?" asked Barir.

"Ancestors?" asked Haniah, giving him a quizzical look.

"Yes, where you're from, your grandparents."

"I don't know," said Haniah. "It's just me, my father, my mother, and my brother."

"No grandparents?"

"Not that I know of," said Haniah.

"That's interesting," Barir grunted.

"What is?"

"Interesting that someone like you would not know your history. You seem well-learned in other things."

"Well, I never really thought about it. And what do you mean 'someone like me?'"

"It's just…there's a familiarity about you."

"Familiarity?"

"It's the way you carry yourself, and the way you speak." He paused and looked at her contemplatively, almost as if he knew something she didn't. "It's probably nothing."

"What's probably nothing?" asked Haniah.

"It's nothing." Barir shrugged. "Forget I said anything about it."

Haniah tugged on Barir's furry arm and spoke sternly. "Tell me what it is."

They sat for a moment, locked in each other's gaze.

"Are you sure your father and mother never told you anything about your ancestry? Where your family is from?"

"We are from the West Hills of Aini."

"That is where I found you. But where was your family from before the West Hills?"

"I don't know," said Haniah quietly and diffidently. Her mind sought for a reason, any reason, why she was never told the answers to Barir's questions.

"That's just interesting." He looked at her deeply. "I wonder what secrets your parents were keeping from you."

"Secrets?" Haniah spoke the word into her chest, but the others heard it under her breath. She looked up into the eyes of her companions. "My family has no secrets. My father and mother told me everything. They wouldn't keep something from me." She became quiet. After all, her father was a guardian and he had never told her that. Somehow, her father had known what a goblin looked like on the night they were attacked. He had never told her how he knew that. She realized there were things she did not know about her parents. Her thoughts began to spiral down. "They just didn't get around to telling me." A frown formed on her face as she looked down at the ground. Haniah's shoulders slumped, and they could see just how upset this conversation had made her.

"That's why it's nothing," said Barir. "I did not mean to upset you."

"Why don't I change the subject?" Ghali's cheerful voice was a stark contrast to the prevailing mood. "I once caught a ground moose by its rear hoof," he said with gusto. He wrestled with his arms as if to demonstrate. "They are the darndest things to catch. You wouldn't believe what I went through to get him. And then, when I did get him, he denied having any part in hiding my underwear." He froze, his arms twisted behind his head, the other two staring blank-faced at him.

"You're weird!" exclaimed Haniah after an uncomfortable silence. Barir let out a hearty bellow of a laugh. Ghali unwound his arms and brought his facial features back to a smile.

"You guys are just way too serious." Ghali got an appreciative pat on the back from Barir. Haniah smiled.

"It's getting dark," said Barir. "Would you like to camp here for the night or continue on? It's a day's journey to the cottage, and if we walked through the night we could make it by late morning."

"I say we keep going," said Haniah, grabbing her things and standing up.

"The note did say to make haste." Ghali finished his last berry. He stood and walked over to a nearby tree. "I say we move on." He picked up a fallen branch and broke off the protruding twigs to create a short straight pole, then handed it to Barir. He did the same to a second branch and handed it to Haniah and made a third for himself. He then cut a deep V shape into the side of a tree with a knife, and they all watched as thick sap slipped from the opening. Ghali struck one end of his pole into the pitch, covering it in sap. From his satchel, Ghali pulled a small iron rod and a small rock. Striking the two together, he produced a spark that caught the sap on his pole and created a flame. He handed his torch to Haniah and then proceeded to do the same to the other two poles.

"I guess we are off then." Ghali led the way south.

The light from the three torches created a halo of light around them, casting dark shadows on the trees and bushes as they passed. The sun had set and all was dark, except the three little lights that passed quietly through the woods.

Haniah followed close to Barir, shifting her gaze back and forth from him to what lay behind her. She couldn't help but imagine trailing goblins and inadvertently kept stepping on his heels. "Are you ok?" asked Barir.

"Who me?" asked Haniah, holding her flame up high as she peered into the dark. "Yeah, why do you ask?"

"You keep bumping into me."

"I'm just a little scared of the dark," she admitted.

"Yes, fear." Barir became philosophical. "Often the anticipation of what is not seen or what could be is worse than the actual truth."

"You sound like my father," said Haniah, still following close behind.

Ghali stopped walking and motioned for the others to hold still. "Did you hear that?"

"Hear what?"

"It's a ways off, but they are coming fast." Ghali's ears perked.

"I can hear it." Haniah held perfectly still. "Sounds like something or somethings running through the brush."

"Oh, no!" said Ghali, grabbing Haniah and pulling her by the arm. "We have to run!"

"What is it?" asked Haniah, trying to keep up.

"Wolves!" Ghali ran with his torch outstretched in front of him.

They had not run far before Haniah could hear the loud growls just behind her. The sounds were much closer than they were a moment ago. A large, black wolf lunged from the dark and slammed into the back of Barir, its fangs bared and jaws snapping. Barir shook the wolf off his back, and the wolf rolled into the bushes. A second clawed at his back, ripping his coat. The wolves targeted his running legs. Haniah dropped her torch as Barir picked her up under his arm and increased his frantic pace, passing the Elver.

A second wolf, larger than its prey, thrust its gaping jaws at Ghali. He stepped on a fallen log and leaped into the air, grabbing a vine that swung him forward, bringing him right in front of Barir. Haniah could hear wolves both behind and to the side of them.

Haniah let out a scream of pain. A wolf had sprung from the forest behind Barir and caught Haniah's leg between its teeth. With a swing of his massive body, Barir yanked Haniah free. The flesh on her thigh tore and burned, making her scream once again in anguish. Barir lifted her limp body up in his open arms. Ghali swung around and hit the wolf in the face with the blunt end of the flaming pole he still carried.

"This way!" yelled Barir. He ran through the brush to a clearing that backed into a cliff wall. He searched for a way around, but didn't find one. The cliff was too steep to climb, especially while carrying such precious cargo. Barir turned back, now facing the direction from which he had come. Ghali followed suit, turning back to face the snarls from the dark.

A dozen sets of gold eyes glistened and circled them, just outside the reach of torch light.

"Barir?" Haniah lifted her head to speak softly.

"Relax." Barir set her down at the foot of the cliff. In the blink of an eye, he shed his backpack, removed his shredded coat, and ripped off the sleeve from his shirt. "This will slow the bleeding." He tied the cloth around Haniah's bleeding leg. "It's going to be ok." The shock from her injury prevented her from registering the panic in his voice.

"Save my family," she said, the strength leaving her body. Black spots mixed with Ghali's waving flame.

"Quick, Barir!" cried Ghali. "There are too many for me to hold off!" He stood between the hungry wolves and the cliff where Haniah lay struggling to stay conscious, waving his torch aggressively.

"I'm thinking!" came Barir's desperate response.

With bared teeth, a wolf made a daring dive past Ghali. Barir braced for the impact. Barir's raised arm suffered a vicious bite before Ghali slammed the hot torch into the wolf's side. A second wolf barreled into Ghali, knocking him down, and his torch slid across the ground. Other wolves quickly followed. Barir cradled Haniah, trying to protect her as the two wolves attacked him unabated. They clamped their jaws onto him and shook viciously, pulling out Barir's fur by the mouthful.

Ghali scooted to place his back against the wall, keeping a worried eye on the encroaching wolves.

The sound of steel pierced through the growls as it sliced through the wolves who had not yet entered the clearing.

Moving in and out of consciousness, Haniah looked out from under Barir and saw a black sword cutting through the beasts in the woods. The wolves cried and whimpered, only to be quieted. The woods became silent as the remaining wolves attempted to escape their killer.

The shadowy form became clearer as their savior advanced on the still-attacking wolves and their weakened prey. A tall and handsome man stepped into the light of the clearing, long sword in hand.

"The hero," whispered Haniah, opening her eyes for the last time, her mouth dry and her vision going black.

The wolves on top of Barir stopped their attack and turned toward the newcomer, forming a circle around him. The man slashed as he spun. The wolves lunged toward him with deadly intent, and the man spun around quickly, slashing his sword at his would-be assassins. They dropped harmlessly to the ground with swift moves from the stranger's sword.

Ghali stared at the dead animals in utter shock, then at the hero who had saved them.

"Where do you travel to?" asked the man.

Barir ignored the question. Frantically, he pulled from his backpack the satchel containing the Blue Gem and stuck it in his pocket.

"We were heading south," said Ghali, coming to himself.

After securing the Blue Gem, Barir quickly moved to place Haniah's satchel containing the White Gem around his neck.

"Not what I asked." The man sheathed his sword.

"We are on our way to get help," said Barir, picking up Haniah in his arms and brushing past the man. "Quick, Ghali. We must go." Barir looked down at the unresponsive Haniah, her legs dangling over his large muscular arms.

"I will travel with you," said the stranger.

"Fine!" Leaving his backpack, Barir ran.

CHAPTER 15

A Meeting of Friends

SHE SAW LIGHT THROUGH HER CLOSED EYELIDS AND KNEW IT WAS day. Haniah opened her eyes and saw that she was in a room with a window, the late morning sun shining through thinly drawn curtains. Warm hues covered the walls, which were made of tightly packed sticks stacked on top of one another. She was struck by the thought that this was probably what it was like to be in a large bird's nest. But of course, it wasn't. There was a porcelain wash bin next to the bed she lay on and a down comforter was tucked tightly around her chest.

Seeing Haniah's open eyes, an old man with a cane moved to Haniah's bedside. "You're awake."

Haniah became light-headed when she tried to sit up.

"Stay where you are." The man placed a hand gently on her shoulder. "You had quite a night. You have lost a lot of blood and will need to regain your strength."

Haniah laid her head back down onto the pillow. A cool rag was placed on her forehead. "My friends," she whispered, her head swimming.

"The large one is here, but he exhausted himself getting *you* here. And good thing he did. If you had lost any more blood, I don't know if you would have made it." Haniah tried to speak before he interrupted her. "Rest. The other two arrived sometime after him and all are being seen to. You will be able to speak with them soon enough."

Relief washed over Haniah's face. "The master of the house looks forward to meeting you when you're feeling better. Here, take this." The man held out a small cup with simmering black liquid inside. Haniah wrinkled her nose at the smell emanating from the cup. "It is something Nuwairah has provided. It will help heal your wounds."

"Is she here?" asked Haniah, trying to sit up again, only to have to lay back down.

"No, she is not. But she did say you would be on your way."

"Was she here?"

"She has been here on occasion, but not for some time." He helped her drink, holding the cup to her lips. "Right now you need to rest, and what I just gave you will help you sleep." He set the cup next to the wash bin, opened the only door to the room, and left.

Haniah closed her eyes and fell into a deep sleep.

❧ ❧

Haniah awoke in a darkened room. A lamp burned low in the corner. A crack of light shone under the door, and she could hear muffled voices on the other side.

Surprisingly, Haniah's strength had returned, and she was able to sit up without feeling dizzy. She walked slowly to the door. Her leg had been bandaged well, but she still felt some pain.

Ghali was the first to notice the door open. He set his cup of tea to the side and stood. Barir looked up from polishing Haniah's sword, his eyes quickly finding the slight figure standing in the doorway.

"She is up." The old man stepped forward to help Haniah into the room. They occupied the front room of a small cottage. An iron stove sat in the corner, a pot of tea steaming on one of the burners.

"Sit here," said the old man, pulling up a chair for her.

"How long have I been asleep?" asked Haniah.

"Two days," answered the old man.

"Two days?" Haniah was astonished. "Feels longer." She placed a hand to her forehead. "I am sorry, I didn't get your name."

"My name is Haqq, and I am at your service." He bowed expertly to Haniah once she was seated.

"Thank you for welcoming us into your home," she said.

"This is not my home. He is the owner." Haqq pointed to an owl Haniah had not noticed before, perched in the corner. "I am merely the caretaker and his mouthpiece." He poured a cup of tea. "You can speak directly to him and thank him yourself."

Haniah looked at the animal in wonder. Large, orange eyes stared back.

"Go ahead. He can understand you," said Haqq as he handed Haniah a cup of tea. "In fact, most animals can understand us. It is humans who are without understanding."

With some hesitation, Haniah spoke to the owl. "Thank you."

The owl tilted its head and blinked its eyes.

"He says, you're welcome."

The owl furrowed the feathers on its head.

"Surprised to see an owl, are you?" translated Haqq.

"No, not exactly. I have seen owls in the trees where I am from, but never thought I would be talking to one. Especially not one so large."

"I imagine you have seen many things of late that you never imagined you would," said Haqq, speaking the words the bird wished.

"That is true." Haniah took a sip of her drink.

Barir gave a soft cough to draw her attention. Haniah looked at him, and he smiled. "How are you feeling?" he asked.

"I am okay. A little tired." She did not mention the pain in her leg and looked around the room once again.

The hero from the other night leaned against one of the roof's support beams. He wore a black cape and his black sword at his side. He stood silent.

"You're the hero Nuwairah the Wizardess sent to save us, aren't you?" asked Haniah.

"Nuwairah the Wizardess?" said the hero. "Aahh…Yes."

"This is my first time meeting a true hero. What is your name?"

"My name is Malak al Maut." The hero placed a hand on his hilt. "Call me Almaut."

"I am honored to make your acquaintance, Almaut," she said, setting her tea on a small table next to her. "Thank you for saving us from the wolves, and thank you for saving me on the night my home was attacked."

"I do my duty." He spoke swiftly and tersely, as though he was now trying to save himself from attention.

"We didn't know if you were going to make it," said Ghali, now sitting in a chair.

"I am glad I did," said Haniah.

"Here, this is yours." Barir handed Haniah her sword. She could see her reflection in the polished steel. "I sharpened the blade with a wet stone and rewrapped the hilt with new leather."

"It's like a brand new sword," said Haniah thankfully. "I didn't think you supported violence."

"I don't. But I do support you," said Barir, giving her a pat on the back.

A rustle of air sounded as the owl spread his feathers and gave two soft flaps of his wings to adjust his position.

"Mr. Pots says there are some matters of business that should be taken care of," said Haqq.

"Mr. Pots?" asked Haniah.

"Yes, that is the owl's name," said Haqq. "Well, not his real name. His animal name cannot be interpreted, so you can call him Mr. Pots."

"What kind of business?" asked Ghali.

The owl leaned forward, lowering his head and raising his back.

"The kingdom is under siege," Haqq spoke. The bird tilted his head to the side, his orange eyes locked on the room's occupants. "Armies of goblins approach the capital Gathbiyya. Something must be done to save it. The king has been gone for many years now and the land has been in need of its rightful ruler."

"How do you know this?" Haniah asked the owl.

"The same way in which I was informed of your arrival. Nuwairah has informed us by way of messengers."

"You say you know Nuwairah?" asked Barir.

"Yes, we both do," said Haqq, speaking for himself. "Our relationships with Nuwairah go back a long way. An intriguing woman. Full of mystery." He rolled his eyes as if remembering something specific. "She gave me this gift, an enchantment that has allowed me to understand the animals."

"Do you know where the wizardess is?" asked Ghali.

"I do not."

"Do you know where she is, Mr. Pots?" Haniah leaned forward, her hands between her knees.

The owl lifted a claw to scratch its beak, and Mr. Haqq translated. "She is on a most important errand."

"Doing what?" asked Almaut sternly. His dark eyes and handsome features seemed to captivate the room. "To find the rightful crown."

"She seeks the king then?" asked Almaut.

"Yes, I believe so, or something like it," said the old man, absently waving his hand as he turned to fill another cup of tea.

"Good. With the king back then he can help with what is going on," said Ghali.

"Some stars are refusing to fade into darkness," said Barir. "That is a good sign. Three hold out. We must hold out as well. Though there be just a few of us, we have to do what we can to help. We have three gems." Barir pulled the satchel containing the White Gem from his pocket and handed it to Haniah.

Almaut shifted on his feet with interest.

"We have one more to find," said Haniah, handing her map to Barir.

Barir unfolded the map and moved to place it on a table against the wall. Ghali and Almaut followed. Haqq stepped close to where Mr. Potts was perched and let him climb onto his shoulder.

"What do we have here?" asked Haqq, moving to look at the map.

"It is a map that shows the location of the four Gems of Anwar," said Barir.

"It appears that the red and final gem is located in the Desert Canyons of Hafiz." Barir placed a finger on the bottom of the map. "It is guarded by something called the Stone of Wisdom."

"The Stone of Wisdom?" asked Ghali. "What is that?"

"I don't know," said Barir. Each of them looked around the room in turn, hoping someone would be able to answer the question.

The owl let out a low hoot, and everyone's attention turned toward him.

"Mr. Pots says there is more written on the map than what you may see," said Haqq, leaning on his cane.

"What is it?" asked Barir.

"Directions."

"To what?" Barir looked intently at the owl.

Mr. Pots opened a silent beak and turned his head to the side. The old man spoke:

"Where does it say that?" asked Almaut abruptly.

"It is written on the map," said Haqq, speaking for the owl. "It's not exactly the type of writing Humans, Elver or Huggars write. It is more like animal tracking than it is reading."

"Animal tracking?" asked Haniah.

"Yes. When tracking an animal, you look at where they have placed their feet, at the trail they have made, or the disturbed foliage. It is much the same with this map. I am not looking at writing per se, but at the location of words and letters, or the imprint of the ink."

"What does it mean?" asked Barir.

The owl shook his head and shrugged his wings.

"It must be talking about magic when it says riches of the world," said Almaut. "What is more valuable than magic?"

Haniah drifted off into her own thoughts as the others talked. She took the locket from around her neck in her hands and opened it. In the glowing circle was the old man, Haqq, and the owl, Mr. Pots. Four green arrows pointed, one each for Barir, Ghali, Haqq, and Mr. Pots. Haniah furrowed her brow as she noticed that no such arrow pointed at the hero, Almaut. Not knowing what it meant and not wanting to draw the others' attention, she discretely placed her necklace under her neckline and continued to listen.

"Do you know how long the journey is from here to the Canyons of Hafiz?" asked Haniah.

"It is at least a seven days journey from here," said the old man, still holding the owl. "I do not think Gathbiyya will hold out that long. The struggle could be over by then."

"Then we should leave as soon as we can," said Ghali.

"Yes, we will retrieve the Red Gem and present all of them at the castle in Gathbiyya," said Barir, turning around to face Haniah. "You will stay here and heal."

"I am coming with you." Haniah used a table at her side to help her stand. "I have not come this far to stay behind. I am up for the trip." She made a fist at her side to show her will and to ease the throbbing in her leg.

"Very well. We will leave now." Barir picked up his mended coat that had been laying over a chair.

The owl turned his head and blinked his eyes. "Mr. Pots says that if you wait until morning, he can expedite your journey."

"By how much?" asked Barir, pausing to listen to the old man.

"Your seven days of travel can be brought down to about two days," said Haqq, once again speaking for the owl. "And it will keep Haniah off that sore leg of hers." He pointed to Haniah's bandaged leg.

"What do you say, Haniah?" asked Barir.

"It sounds good to me." She looked at the others.

Ghali confirmed his approval, and Almaut gave a single nod.

"Then our minds are made up," said Barir. "We will stay the night and leave tomorrow morning."

Haniah ate two bowls of soup and crackers, then retired to her room to sleep. Barir, Ghali, and Almaut made bedding around the iron stove, and Haqq slept in a hammock strung from one wall to another. Perched up above, the owl kept a watchful eye throughout the night.

❧ ❦

In the morning, they ate a breakfast of nuts and berries mixed with milk. They packed their bags, each guardian carried a satchel containing a gem. Haqq, with Mr. Pots on his shoulder, walked them some distance from the cottage. Haniah looked back at the cottage and saw blue smoke coming from the chimney. The stove inside still burned.

Haqq stopped them at the edge of a grove of trees and walked a few paces forward. Mr. Pots gave a hoot that pierced the still morning air.

A few moments later, the head of a giant fox brushed through tree limbs as it saunterd out from the tree line. It was the height of two horses, standing one upon the other. Silently it approached, bushy tail trailing behind.

"No sudden movements. She is likely to think you're food," said Haqq. To the fox, they were about the size of mice. The fox took graceful steps to the old man and the owl. Haqq reached high above his head to place his hand delicately to the fox's lowered nose. The fox smelled the man and gently nuzzled the owl. Without turning his back to the fox, he motioned for the others to come forward. Haniah felt its breath blow through her hair as the fox took its time inspecting each of them. "Her name is Sishu, and she will carry you to your destination."

The fox lowered herself close to the ground, and one by one they climbed aboard her back. Once she was settled, Haniah admired the softness of the animal's vibrant red fur between her fingers.

Within moments everyone was on board, and the fox started running back through the grove from which it appeared.

Haniah watched as the land passed by. It was like a dream. She had not imagined the world could fly by as it did. The fox followed gullies and ridge lines that crossed the land. The ride felt natural to Haniah, and she could tell the fox would not let anyone see them unless she wanted them to. Haniah felt exhilarated and as free as the wind blowing in her hair.

Barir's face turned green with every rise and drop of the land. Ghali rode like he was born for it, with perfect balance, a grin on his face. Almaut showed no pleasure from this unexpected mode of transport, but neither did he show any displeasure. His was a face of placid indifference.

They watched as the world transitioned from lush greens to dry, sandy browns and oranges. For two days and two nights the fox ran, stopping only twice to let them rest and eat. At the entrance of the Canyons of Hafiz was a river, with high cliff walls to either side. The fox slowed, letting her travelers climb down from her back. She left as she came, only a whisper of sound marking her departure. She did not communicate any message and did not wait for a thank you. Haniah watched the fox disappear into the haze in the distance.

CHAPTER 16

Death

THEY FOLLOWED THE RIVER THAT RAN THROUGH THE CENTER OF the winding, narrow canyon. Sunlight streamed into the canyon and illuminated the cliff walls like a bright, orange fire. The summer warmth felt nice on Haniah's arms and face. Still walking with a slight limp, she followed her companions for several hours before they came to a large arch made of rock. Under the arch was a trailhead that twisted and turned its way up the canyon wall.

"I believe this is it." Barir, who was leading the way, stopped to check on the others, though his main purpose was to check on Haniah. "This should be the trail to the Stone of Wisdom and the Red Gem." Haniah rested against a boulder. Ghali leaned down at the river's edge and washed his hands and face.

Almaut moved between the others and the arch. "This is where your journey ends," he hissed with an evil look in his eyes. A funnel of swirling black smoke began to form above his head and moved down to engulf his entire body as he drew his long black sword. His handsome face transformed into a hideous skull with dark, hollow eye sockets. Sinuous wings unfurled from behind his back. Smoke bubbled at his feet. No light reflected from off his black armored body. When the smoke settled, Haniah no longer saw a man. It was Death walking.

"A specter!" roared Barir

Haniah backed away from the boulder she had been standing against. Ghali jumped up into a defensive stance.

"So, you know what I am," hissed the specter, a crooked grin on his face. "I am willing to make you a deal." Barir took a step back, and Haniah moved to stand behind the boulder. "I will let one of you live. I seek the Golden Gem. The first one who tells me where to find it will live."

None spoke.

"Come now. Do you not wish to save yourself?" He pointed the long tip of his razor sharp sword at Ghali.

"We don't know where it is." Ghali took a step back into the water. "You know as much as we do about where to find it."

"Don't talk to him, Ghali," said Barir. "He has no intention of letting one of us go."

"How wise you are, Huggar," he sneered.

"You saw what he did to the wolves," said Barir. "Don't get close to him."

"If you do not tell me what I wish, then you shall die."

Barir did not answer. Haniah's heart jumped and pounded in her throat. Ghali stood in the river with the water up to his boots.

"Have it your way." He spat out the words with vile anger as he charged. "You shall be the first to die." Barir ducked the swinging sword and rolled across the dusty ground. The specter swiveled around to face Barir, who was now standing ready for the specter's next move. He let out a sneer as he swept his wings into the air and took a flying leap toward the Huggar. Barir dodged again. Quick as lightning, the specter swung his sword and lunged a third and final time. Barir, barely able to catch his breath, rolled again across the ground, but not quickly enough. The specter's blade ran through his side. Barir let out a painful roar. The specter slowly removed his poison tipped blade and Barir fell to his knees, his body collapsing to the floor. The specter raised his sword above Barir's head to finish his deadly deed.

The clang of iron echoed through the canyon as Haniah's raised sword stopped the specter's sword in mid-flight. A flurry of reflective light splashed above Barir's bleeding body as Haniah's polished steel danced with the specter's black blade. The specter was far quicker and much more deadly than Haniah, and she backed down with each powerful swing. "You're no match for me, child. Your friend is dead and so you shall be," the creature cackled. Haniah's leg ached with each blow and her body shook. Her strength was no match for the specter, and she knew she was beat. She closed her eyes and braced for death.

Ghali drew back on his magic bow, and a glowing arrow appeared, already notched, near Ghali's cheek. "Get down!" The Elver's voice sang in Haniah's ears as she dropped to the ground, just as the arrow raced to save her life.

The arrow flew over her head, piercing the specter's dark armor in the center of his chest. A glorious explosion of light radiated from the specter's black armor. In his agony, the specter dropped his black sword into the dirt with a clang. He took one unbalanced step backward, then stumbled to the ground where he lay unmoving. Smoke gathered around the specter's body, forming a whirlwind that disintegrated his body, leaving behind a black stain where the specter once lay.

Haniah ran over to Barir and slid to the ground next to her dying friend. With effort, he opened his eyes and spoke. "Do you remember our conversation on the mountaintop?" Haniah helped lift his head onto her knee.

"Don't talk," she said.

"It is not only the evil of the world we have fought, but ourselves," he said, pain written on his face.

"Water!" she said as she turned to Ghali. "Get him water—I think he needs water." Turning back to Barir, she spoke in earnest. "Don't talk. You're losing blood and you need your strength."

"I must, while I still can. I can feel the cold burn of the poison move through my veins." He took a shallow, ragged breath and grimaced in pain. "The fight for greatness within ourselves…" he paused to cough. A spasm of pain rippled through his body. "I fight for the greatness that lies within us, as I do for that which lies within our foes."

Ghali brought a canteen filled with water from the river, and Haniah poured it over Barir's lips. The young girl looked intently on the face of the great beast.

Barir's emotion-filled eyes burrowed deep within Haniah's soul. His voice came out soft and weak. "I tried to change us all for the better. But now I must go. The rest is up to you." The words barely passed his lips as he coughed.

"I don't know how to change things." Haniah leaned in to hold him close. "How am I supposed to change things? I can't even change this!" she cried.

Haniah ran her hand across her friend's forehead. She could see he was in pain. He choked back a grimace on his face before speaking again. "Tell my son and wife I love them." He whispered the words and closed his eyes. Haniah felt the tension in his muscles leave. Life left Barir's body.

"No! No, this isn't happening." Frantically, she placed her hand upon his face in the hopes of getting a response. "You have to stay! You can't die!"

She looked around her from side to side. "Quick, where is my satchel?" She hastily laid Barir's head on the ground and scrambled to the place where the satchel lay.

Holding the White Gem above Barir's body, she willed the gem to work with as much force as she could muster. A faint light began to glow from the gem, but faded quickly. She tried harder, tightening her grip on the gem and pressing it against her chest. "Work!" she cried. Nothing. He did not move. "Wake up!" she sobbed, shaking his shoulders. Her desperation heightened as she threw her arms over him and buried her face in his chest. Shortly, her desperation turned to grief and despair.

"He's gone, Haniah." Ghali placed a hand on her shoulder. She turned around and slid to sit in the dirt, her back against Barir, her face in her hands.

"I have to get to the Stone of Wisdom," said Haniah, lifting her head from her hands with new energy. "The Stone of Wisdom will know what to do." She placed the gem in its satchel, picked up her sword, and made her way to the trail's head. Once under the stone arch, she ran.

CHAPTER 17

Stone of Wisdom

L OOKING DOWN AT THE WINDING CANYON NOW FAR BELOW HER, Haniah paused to catch her breath. For a moment, she was able to take in the splendor of the magnificent scenery before setting off at a run that quickly turned to a laborious hike. The trail was steep with switchbacks and life-threatening drops. Haniah was careful to stay to the side of the trail closest to the cliff wall.

Tight curls of hair clung to the sweat on her forehead, and she had to periodically wipe her brow with the short sleeve of her dress. Her leg ached, but she pressed on.

The trail narrowed at the top of a ridge that led to a plateau high above the other rock formations. Haniah grabbed hold of an iron rod that was anchored between two stones to help her walk across the section of loose rock. The bronze that once covered the iron had long been rubbed off. The footing of rock underneath was uneven, and the first stone she placed her weight on gave way. Grabbing tightly to the iron rod, she saved herself from the deadly fall. Her legs dangled over the ledge as she watched broken stone tumble out of sight. She situated her feet on a flat rock and carefully moved along the length of the ridge, all the more intent upon holding fast to the iron rod.

Upon reaching the safety of the plateau, she wiped her wind-blown hair from her face. Blue sky and painted white clouds passed behind a mammoth-sized carving of a head that dwarfed Haniah.

"Welcome to the Temple of Wind." The statue's lips moved with a deep rumble, stone grinding against stone. "To you, this will be sacred ground. What is your desire?"

"Can you save my friend?" she said. "He was stabbed by a specter's sword."

"No," came the sad reply. "I cannot. I am a statue. I understand you attempted to save him using a Gem of Anwar. If the gem could not do it, surely I cannot."

"Why did it not work?"

"You do not possess the ability of bringing someone back to life. The gem can only enhance the abilities one already has."

"Can the Red Gem be used to save him?" asked Haniah. She didn't want to believe what he was saying.

"The Red Gem has been stolen."

"By whom?"

"By an evil wizard named Amjad Fatih." The statue looked down at Haniah. "It was taken a summer ago. You may have noticed the world becoming dark and the stars refusing to shine. He has spent the past season creating an army of goblins and dark wings. He now seeks the other three gems, the three gems you and your friend have. Once he has them, he will cover the world with despair."

"What can you do to stop it?"

"I am a statue, my abilities are limited. What I do have is wisdom."

"I don't need wisdom!" Haniah raised her voice in frustration. Her hands were shaking. "What I need is something to save my friend!" Haniah reached into her satchel, pulled out the White Gem, and held it up to the statue. "These are useless!" The statue said nothing. "You're useless!" She shook her fist at the on-looking stone.

"The gems are only as useful as the one who guards them." The statue spoke in a steady, even tone.

"Then I am useless." She turned her back to the Stone of Wisdom and looked back down the difficult path she had taken to get there.

"Don't say that."

"What do you know?" she snapped, turning back to face the statue. "How can you even be a guardian if you are a stone statue? You can't even fight off someone who comes to take something from you! We're both useless." Her disgust with the statue mixed with her despair. "If you had been stronger, if you'd been able to protect the Red Gem, my family would not have been attacked. He used it to take them from me." Haniah dropped to her knees and hugged her belly in anguish.

"Knowledge is knowing something, but knowing the right way to use that knowledge is wisdom."

"Riddles?" Haniah spoke into the dirt.

"It is advice." He continued, "Let happen what will happen. No need to fight it. No need for defenses. No need for struggle. Everything balances out in the end. Injustice may reign for a time, but the scales of justice always tip back to fairness. Your friend knew this."

Haniah felt sick. It lingered in her stomach. The pain and confusion of not being able to do anything, of being powerless, made her insides turn. She pounded her fist against the rocky outcrop. Dust stirred, but the solid ground did not move. Barir was solid. Solid, stable, and strong like the canyon rocks. She had seen him take the full brunt of a dragon's tail. He had carried her through the night and saved her life. She longed to feel his soft fur against her cheek. She remembered how she grew tired of eating roots day after day, and how he continued loving them, meal after repetitious meal. She missed his silly grin and the way he winked his eye at her.

His memory brought a tear to her eye. It slid down her cheek and fell onto the dusty ground. Her tear was not alone. The sky had darkened, and clouds moved in. The rain started a few drops at a time, speckling the ground around her. The dry ground was soon wet.

"Let the tears flow," the statue said. Haniah's shoulders shook as she cried. "Drink it in deeply." With his permission, her sobs came unabated. "Like the cinnamon in a cake, feelings are the spice of life."

Haniah looked down at the ground. Wet strands of hair hung in her face, and water dampened her clothes as she sat in the rain. She ran her hands across her reddened cheeks to clear her sight. *Cinnamon in a cake?* The words brought memories to her mind. Thoughts came of her mother's caring smile. She remembered her mother teaching her how to write her letters. She could see her mother standing at the oven in the cottage, baking. Her mind was taken back to the time she sat eating cinnamon cake on the side of the road, alone. Of the time she drank the milk Nuwairah had given her, telling her to drink deeply.

Haniah looked up from the wet stone slab she sat on and stared the statue in the eye. "How do you know about the cinnamon cake?"

"I am the Stone of Wisdom. There is much that I know. Knowing is not the important part. The important part is knowing what to do with what we know."

"What do you mean when you say 'drink it in deeply?'" she said, now willing to listen.

"What are riches?" asked the stone. Haniah stood staring at the statue, tired of questions and seeking answers. "Could it be said that it is a gem? Is it gold? Money? A good time? A fleeting moment of pleasure?" The statue raised an eyebrow. "Maybe riches to you is a jeweled crown upon your head and a kingdom to rule?" The statue paused as though to wait for her response. None came but an eager look from the young girl. "I tell you, the riches of the world are not rubies or gold. To some it is. But to the wise it is not. True treasures are the feelings of joy, love, and happiness." The statue paused again, with a little gentleness added to his voice. "Sorrow is also a treasure of the world that should not be overlooked. Sorrow shows you have heart. Deep sorrow shows you have love. These things you should drink deeply. Like the things you eat, they nourish and strengthen you." The statue gave as much of a smile as any stone statue could before speaking again. "Do you understand?"

"You're saying it's okay to cry?"

"Yes, I am. It is okay to cry." Haniah let a corner of her lip turn up. "It is good that you learn this. Those who feel with their heart have true strength and power. There is nothing worse than an apathetic one. And nothing greater than a loving one."

Haniah looked up at the statue with a puzzled look. "Apathetic?"

"An apathetic person is one who does not care. They are callous and cold. If you did not care for your family like you do, if you did not care for your friend as you do, you would not have this sorrow. It shows you have a pure heart. I do not need any Huggar aid or a Huggar magic locket to see that in you." Haniah touched the magic necklace around her neck.

"You say my feelings show that I have a good heart?" Haniah sat up on her knees.

"Yes. You, my young girl, hold the riches of the world within your heart. If you follow what is in your heart, you will always find that you have enough strength for what you seek."

"I am glad you think I have a good heart, but what can having a good heart do for me now? My friend has been killed, and my family is missing."

"Much worse will happen without the likes of you. You must get what gems you have to the castle and do everything in your power to get the Red Gem from the one who stole it. Then the kingdom will have a chance of being saved, and you may find what a good heart can do."

"And Barir?" Haniah looked down at the canyon floor in the direction of her fallen friend.

"I am sorry. He has made his choice and is unable to be saved," he said solemnly.

"This isn't fair. This isn't the way it's supposed to be."

"I agree. It is not fair, but it very well may be the way it is supposed to be," said the stone. "Barir would not wish you to stop here. He died so you could go on." Haniah wiped at her eyes and took a deep breath. "You need to be going. Travel swiftly. There is still hope for your family," said the statue.

Haniah rose to her feet, turned away from the statue and walked slowly back down the way she had come. She walked dejectedly, her head low. She saw no need to hurry, as there was no life on the line, no one to save. Her friend was dead, and she felt empty.

When she reached the canyon floor, she saw Ghali look up at her as she walked back under the arch. Barir's body had been moved. The lines in the sand from where he had been dragged had been washed away by the rain. Ghali had used one of the large crevices along the canyon wall to house her friend's body. He rolled the last of the boulders into place to seal the grave.

"I didn't want you to have to do it," said Ghali, referring to Barir's burial. Haniah walked past him without saying anything and knelt down at the foot of the stones. "I'll let you be alone." He walked down to the river to give Haniah her privacy.

Before she could get words out to say her goodbye, a screech sounded from above. A shifting black mass with a thousand limbs blocked out the light that shone through the clouds.

Ghali noticed the change first. "Haniah!" he yelled. "Take cover!" The black figures descended on them like spilled ink. The winged monsters attacked with gnashing teeth and outstretched claws. One monster

grabbed Haniah and lifted her off the ground, flapping its raven-feathered wings. Ghali ran to her, drawing and releasing a volley of light arrows from his bow, striking the creature in its heart. Haniah dropped, and Ghali picked her up from off the ground. "Quick, climb into that crevice in the rock!" More creatures attacked, and more arrows flew. Haniah squeezed into the crack in the rock and tucked herself as far back as she could.

Dark flyers clambered into the opening where Haniah hid, climbing the walls like rabid roaches and biting the stone in an attempt to get at her. Haniah tried to slap the clawed hands away, but there were too many. She was pulled from her hiding place and lifted into the air. Kicking and screaming, she called for Ghali to help her, but Ghali was cornered and hiding in the rocks. The higher she flew, the smaller the valley became. She struggled to free herself until she was exhausted and unable to fight any more. She was passed in midflight from one monster to another.

The monsters flew north from where she was captured, over the desert, over rolling hills covered with fields to the center of the kingdom. Far below, she saw the dark masses of armies strung out over the world in long lines, marching in the direction of the kingdom's capital. The sun was preparing to set when they arrived at their destination—a fifty thousand goblin army, set at a siege against Gathbiyya.

Outside the protection of the city wall were the burnt remains of inns, homes, stores and other wood structures that had been built with the support of the city. The encroaching army had not left any building unscathed. Three hundred paces from the charred ground, and outside the reach of a bow, was the goblins' first line of encampment. Tents and goblins encircled the entire city. Their filth, grime, and rank smells ran the length of their muddy, filthy camp.

In contrast, the white walls of the castle reflected the gold light of the setting sun like a great beacon amidst its current surroundings. If not for Haniah's situation, she would have found the castle towers majestic and inspiring with its violet spires. Instead, all she could focus on was the dark, filthy camp she was being lowered to below.

CHAPTER 18

Goblins and Grocks, Oh My

THERE WAS A RUSTLE OF SOUND ACROSS THE ROOM, LIKE SOMEONE rummaging through a stack of parchment or handling a folded map. She heard something soft being thrown against the side of the tent. The smell of rotting flesh permeated the air, and mud and sweat crowded her nostrils.

Haniah stayed still and kept her eyes closed. She could feel the tent post against her back and the ropes they used to tie her hands to the pole behind her. There was no getting away. She had been trying to find a way to free herself for the past two days. The ropes were too tight, and she was out of hope.

"Do we have to keep holding on to this thing?" asked a gruff goblin voice.

"Master wants it," said a second, deeper voiced goblin. "It should bring us a great reward."

"Fresh meat to eat?" She heard a thump as one of the goblins placed what he had been holding back on the table. The White Gem. They had taken it from her. The gruff sounding goblin moved toward her and snatched her hair in his fisted fingers. "How about this meat, can we eat it?"

"We can't eat her yet." The deep sounding goblin moved closer to where Haniah sat.

"We can put her in our stew and no one will know the better of it." He yanked her head up by her hair. Haniah could smell the creature's rank breath, but she remained focused on keeping her eyes closed and body limp.

"Master will know," said the deep voice. "I sent him a message once the grocks brought her in."

"Where is he?" The hand holding her head let go with a shake. Haniah let her chin drop to her chest. She had listened to the two voices for over a period of two days, pretending to be unconscious. But she had not been able to sleep. In listening to the two goblins' banter, she discerned that one was the General of the camp. The one with the deeper voice was captain of the guard, subordinate to the General.

"He is out looking for the rest of these things," said the goblin General. "He will be here when we take the castle."

"Well, don't let any more of the goblins know we have her," said the captain of the guard. "I want to add her to my stew, and there isn't enough of her to go around for everyone."

"*Your* stew?" grumbled the General.

"I get her!" argued the captain. "I am the one who found her."

"No, you're not!" fired back the General. He gave an open-handed slap upside the back of the captain's head. "The grocks found her."

"Yeah, but I was the first to see her after they brought her here," said the captain, with a punch to the General's face. Haniah heard the two taking and giving their best blows. Their noisy ruckus spilled out of the tent and into the muddy walkways of the camp. "Come back here, you coward!" the General yelled, chasing after the captain until their voices were out of range of Haniah's hearing.

Haniah took a deep breath and let her eyes slowly open. The tent she was being kept in was now empty of threats. She had been faking unconsciousness for two days to avoid interacting with the crude creatures. She also avoided her feelings, fearing that she couldn't keep herself from falling apart. Her friend, Barir, was dead. Before she could even mourn his loss, she was captured by flying creatures called grocks and deserted by the only companion she had left, Ghali. She had been warned by the Elver King that Ghali would desert her, and she blamed herself completely for her situation. She should have known better, or done something differently. What that was exactly, she did not know. But she should have done something. She hated to imagine that things could get any worse, so she avoided any other thoughts and sat like a rag doll, pretending to be unconscious. She attempted to keep her emotions in check, numb to the world around her.

She heard footsteps outside the tent flap and quickly closed her eyes and dropped her head. The tent flap opened. She could barely hear a pair of boots lightly shuffling across the floor toward her—too light to be goblin boots. They walked to where she was tied and knelt down in front of her. To her surprise, there was no smell of rot or bad breath. Instead, she was met with the pleasant smell of sweet berries. The person wearing the boots was silent, almost as if waiting for Haniah to move. Timidly, she opened one eye. "Ghali!"

"Shhh." Ghali placed a finger to his lips to keep her quiet. "They will hear you." He moved to her back and loosened the ropes enough so she could free her hands. "Here, I brought you these." He held up a handful of sweet berries. Without hesitation, Haniah grabbed them and shoved them all into her open mouth. "Yeah, I didn't think they would have fed you." He looked her over for injuries. Aside from being tired and hungry, she seemed to be okay. The bandage on her leg was still there.

Haniah looked at Ghali's welcome face in astonishment. "I didn't think you would come for me. Your parents said you were a deserter."

"Can't believe everything they say," he said with half a smile. "I am so glad you're alive. I feared you were dead. As soon as they took you, I came running after you."

"How did you get in here?" asked Haniah.

"It's the Green Gem!" He stood up and held the gem out to her. "It makes me practically invisible to these brutes. The Blue Gem doesn't seem to do anything for me." He patted the satchel containing the Blue Gem. His ears perked up as he listened for sounds outside the tent. "This place is crawling with goblins, and the castle is under siege."

"How are we getting out of here?" asked Haniah, walking over to pick up the White Gem that had been left on the table. She placed it in her satchel along with her father's map and picked up her sword that had also been placed on the table.

"I don't know," said Ghali. "I only thought about how I would get in." They heard heavy boots outside the tent. "Quick, someone is coming." They moved to stand at both sides of the doorway. Ghali placed the Green Gem in the pocket opposite the Blue Gem he carried. When the goblin General entered the tent, Ghali jumped into action. He threw his satchel over the goblin's head. Blinded and confused, the goblin was taken completely by surprise. In an act of desperation, the Elver jumped on its back, his arms wrapped tightly around the goblin's neck, causing the monster to go into a frantic spasm, clawing and hitting. "Help!" yelled Ghali. The goblin rolled onto its back, smashing Ghali to the ground. "Help," he called again, breathless, the air having been knocked out of his lungs.

Haniah lifted her sword into the air and brought down the hilt on the goblin's helmet-covered head with all the force she could muster. The goblin rolled off Ghali and stopped moving. "Good golly!" said Ghali, brushing himself off as he stood. He gave the fallen monster a nudge with his foot. It did not move. "I didn't expect that."

"It was remarkably more effective than I had anticipated as well," said Haniah, inspecting the hilt of her sword.

Without warning, a second goblin stood inside the tent door, gasping audibly. Before the captain of the goblin guard could make a move or call for help, Ghali dove for his feet and brought them both tumbling to the ground. Haniah jumped on its head, shoved a handful of cut rope into its open mouth, and handed the rest to her companion. Ghali quickly tied one end around the wrists of the fighting goblin and the other end to its ankles. Once Haniah had finished tying the rope securely inside the goblin's mouth, she climbed off its head and looked proudly at their handiwork. The goblin twisted and squirmed in an attempt to escape the tight ropes.

"How many goblins know you're here?" asked Ghali.

"Just these two and all the grocks that brought me here," said Haniah "These two are the only ones who have been guarding me."

"Let's hope no more come in." Ghali stepped over the goblin bodies. "There is only so much floor space in here." He wrinkled his nose. "And only so much goblin smell I can handle." He peered outside the tent through a thin opening in the tent's door flap. "We still have to figure out how to get out of here."

As she looked around the room, Haniah's attention was drawn to the unconscious goblin and its armor. "Here, put this on." She removed the general's helmet from its head and handed it to Ghali.

"This is a very creative idea," he said, putting on the helmet to cover his face.

"My father always did tell me I have an active imagination." Haniah took the armor off of the struggling goblin and placed it on herself.

"I think this just might work." Ghali stood back to look at Haniah who was now dressed in a black breastplate and was putting on a pair of large boots. "You're a little small for a goblin, and I am a little tall, but from what I have seen of these things, they aren't very bright." Ghali pulled on a big leather glove. "After all, it's been two days and they haven't been able to figure out that you have been faking sleep." He smiled, and she smiled back. "I think I know you better than you think I know you." He gave her a wink with his eye, a wink that resembled one Barir would have given her. She was glad to still have her friend, Ghali, with her.

The rain had stopped by the time Haniah and Ghali stepped out of the tent, but the remaining mess of mud and goblin sweat stuck to their boots. Ever since Haniah had visited the Stone of Wisdom, it had continued to rain off and on. Now, the clouds broke, and rays of light could be seen streaming down upon the world.

"Wait," Ghali said to Haniah as she made to saunter off among the tents.

"What?" she asked.

"You can't walk like you normally do." He leaned close to the canvas of the tent they had just come from and spoke softly. "You have to hunch your back or something."

"There. Does that work?" She leaned over with one shoulder higher than the other, letting her lower arm hang.

"That's much better," he said. "But something else is still missing." He scratched his head. "I got it! You don't smell like a goblin either."

"What do you propose I do about that?" she asked, shifting her weight and placing a hand on her hip. Ghali looked pointedly at her and then down at the mud she stood in. "Oh no! I am not doing that."

"Do you want to get out of here or don't you?" countered Ghali. "I'll have to do it too."

"Fine." The mud squelched as she lowered herself onto her knees.

"You have to do more than that."

"Well, why don't you get down here and see how you like it? This stuff is disgusting." She lifted a handful of the grime and watched it ooze through her closed fingers.

Ghali held his breath as he got down on his knees and rolled around in the mud, covering himself from head to toe in filth. Haniah rolled as well before getting back onto her feet. Uncomfortable, they looked at one another. The only white that could be seen on their bodies was the white in their eyes.

"You missed a spot," said Ghali, smearing a handful of mud across Haniah's already dirty cheek.

"You did that just to do it." Haniah gave him her best glare.

"That's a good goblin look," he said with a gleeful smile as Haniah stepped past him to lead the way. Ghali struggled not to giggle.

"I am not laughing," she replied without looking back. Mud dripped off her goblin armor.

They snaked their way through a camp made up of fire pits and tents, heading in the general direction of the castle. They passed a giant catapult crudely made from lumber and iron. It was obvious to Haniah that whoever designed it was clearly not one of the goblins before her. She watched as several of them jumped and pushed on the catapult to release it from the mud and move it to the front line. One goblin chewed helplessly on a giant wooden wheel, and another pushed in the wrong direction.

"Watch where you're going!" barked a goblin. He passed by Haniah and hit shoulders with her, almost knocking her off her feet.

"Excuse me," grumbled Haniah in her best goblin voice. She pressed forward, and found herself at a campfire inside a circle of tents. Twenty or so goblins gathered around the fire. Haniah looked for a way around, but saw none. She continued through the crowd of goblins to get to the other side when one grabbed her around the neck with its bicep.

"Yar! Have a drink." The goblin handed her a large mug and pushed her down next to a line of goblins, all sitting on a fallen pole. "You too, you worm." He grabbed Ghali by the shoulder, handed him a mug, and shoved him down next to Haniah. Around them the goblins drank, laughed, and hit one another on the back of the head. A few sang songs while holding mugs high above their heads, the contents spilling out with each jostle and sway of their bodies. Their speech was so garbled that Haniah could not make out the words to the song, and she wondered if it could truly even be considered music. Whatever they were about, the goblins seemed to be enjoying themselves, and to Haniah's amusement, were quite oblivious to the two escapees sitting in their midst.

Haniah looked down into her cup. Dark, bubbly liquid filled the mug. She leaned her nose in close and breathed in, then pulled a face with her tongue sticking out. She recognized the smell from when the captain of the guard breathed on her. It was rank on his breath then and rank in the cup now.

"Don't drink it," said Ghali, leaning over so only she could hear. "It's fermented."

"Fermented?" asked Haniah.

"Rotten apples and who knows what else." He shrugged his shoulder in the direction of all the goblins and spoke under his breath. "They are drunk." He nonchalantly placed his mug at his feet. Haniah poured hers out behind her back and placed the empty mug on the ground.

"Done already?" said the goblin, looking at her empty mug. He grabbed her by the wrist and walked her to the campfire. "We just started cookin' up some tasty stew." Haniah looked into the cauldron the goblins had hung above the fire. She looked more closely at the solid masses in the boiling liquid until she realized what it was. Bobbing heads.

"Oh my!" she gasped, stepping back from the boiling pot.

"We found these ones just outside the city walls." The goblin knocked her on the back. "Already dead, not fresh, but beggars can't be choosers." He grinned, revealing his razor sharp teeth. "Stick around and you can have some." He wiped his slobbering mouth on a tattered and dirty sleeve.

Haniah tasted bile but managed to swallow it back down, and took her seat next to Ghali. "We have to get out of here." She looked around for a way out. About fifty paces behind the goblins, a grock sat, tearing apart limbs from something dead, biting and tearing at the carcass with its razor teeth. Seeing the grock sitting away from the circle of goblins, she realized something. *Not even grocks can stand the smell of goblins.* "Don't those things have any table manners?" she asked out loud.

"What is that you say?" asked a goblin nearby. "Table manners? What kind of goblin are you?" The goblin opened one eye more than the other to get a better look at her and her mud-covered face.

"I mean, that looks like a yummy piece of dead meat." She lowered her voice and grunted.

"Table manners!" exclaimed the brute, giving Haniah a jab with its elbow, right into her ribs. "You had me going there. You're a funny one." He eyed her closer. "What is this?" He looked down at the blue hem of her dress sticking out from under her armor. "You're wearing color?" The goblin stood and ripped the padded goblin pants Haniah wore, revealing her blue skirt beneath. "A dress? You're wearing a dress?" The other goblins in the circle stopped singing, looked at Haniah and then at one another. Haniah could almost see the little wheels in their heads trying to puzzle out what they were seeing, all asking themselves the same question—why is a goblin wearing a dress?

"Boy, are they dumb," said Ghali. The goblins continued to sit and stare. Getting up from his seat, he strode through the dumbfounded crowd. He waved his hand for Haniah, and she quickly followed. The grock stopped chewing and looked at the bright blue color moving through the congestion of bewildered goblins. The grock spread its wings. With jaws open wide and fangs extended, the dark creature leaped into the air at the pair. Ghali released a white light arrow that pierced the charging monster square between the eyes. The grock landed dead at Ghali's feet with a crash and a splatter of mud. One of the wings tipped over the cauldron of boiling heads, which sent all the goblins into a rage.

"That's your cue to run, Haniah!" Ghali yelled, drawing back his bow and striking several goblins in a quick succession of arrows. "I'll cover you!"

A cry arose from surrounding grocks as the camp went into a frenzy, all focused on catching Ghali and Haniah. Haniah ran past Ghali, through a line of tents, onto an open plane that stretched toward the castle.

Ghali shot the next dozen goblins who attacked, but he was clearly outnumbered. Ghali turned and quickly followed after Haniah.

Haniah ran with a slight limp. She shed the heavy breast plate and large gloves to make running easier. A black mass of grocks and goblins began to pour out of the dark campground behind. "Open the gates!" she yelled to the watchmen standing on the city walls. But they were still too far to hear her plea.

"Duck!" Ghali yelled to Haniah. She dove to the ground just as a large, black claw reached out to grab her from above. Ghali released another arrow, sending the monster tumbling into the field. It landed with an explosion of dirt and grass. Ghali lifted her by the arm and they continued their run. "We can do this, Haniah! Keep going!"

৵৵

"What is this?" asked one of the guards. He wore a polished silver helmet and was perched high up on the city wall of Gathbiyya.

"What is what?" asked a companion soldier. The first pointed to the field laid out before them with an outstretched arm. "There!" On the plane between the city and the dark camp beyond were two figures running some distance in front of a charging horde of fifty goblins and dark flyers.

"Are they attacking?" asked the soldier.

"I don't think so. There aren't enough of them," replied the first. "Sounds like the two in front are saying something." He held his ear in the direction of the yelling figures. "I think they are calling for us to lower the drawbridge."

"Are they goblins?"

"I don't think so. They don't run like goblins, and they certainly don't sound like them."

"Well, whoever they are, it looks like they could use some help."

"Lower the gate!" yelled the guard down to some soldiers far below. "Archers, at attention!" he called to the line of resting archers laying against the wall's battlements.

The door came down, and both Ghali and Haniah ran into the city. The chasing goblins and grocks retreated back from the defending arrows shot by the Gathbiyya guards on the city wall.

CHAPTER 19

Sieged

THE MANY YEARS HANIAH SPENT RUNNING FROM THE POND TO THE family farm house had proven invaluable. She was safe inside the city. Both she and Ghali leaned over with their hands on their knees, taking deep breaths to recover from their run. The heavy fortress doors closed behind them.

"Who are you?" came a stern voice. A man dressed in shining armor and a violet cape stood before them. He wore an insignia with wings spread wide on his breastplate and held a chrome helmet with a plume of feathers under his arm. Other knights around him wore the same attire, with the exception of the violet cape.

"This is Haniah, and I am Ghali." He gestured to Haniah then tipped his hat at the men and women before them. "We are guardians of the Gems of Anwar. I am the guardian of the Green Gem." He reached into his pocket and pulled out the gem he had received in the tower of Shahirah.

The armored knights bent down on one knee and placed a fist to the ground, heads lowered to the gem. Ghali gave Haniah a puzzled look.

"Please stand up," said Haniah. "We are here to help. We must present the gems at the castle where the Golden Gem will then be revealed."

The knight with the cape rose from the ground and pushed his cape behind his shoulder. "I am Abdul, captain of the winged guards of

Gathbiyya." He spoke gravely. "I am not sure how much even you can help. Walk with me." He turned and began his walk up a cobbled road that led to the castle. Haniah and Ghali followed close behind, and the other knights disbanded to other areas of the fortress. They walked at a quick pace, with Haniah skipping a step now and again to keep up.

The street was clean, with shops and inns lining its sides. People kept to their homes, their doors and windows locked, leaving the road to the men and women dressed for battle. A group of knights tended to what looked like giant birds gathered in a stable yard. They had feathers, wings, and a beak, but that seemed to be all they had in common with the birds Haniah knew. They had large black eyes, front arms with claws, and a long tail with a tuff of fur on the end. She noticed one knight sitting astride the smallest creature's back.

"What are those?" asked Haniah as they passed by.

"Those are ott flyers," responded Captain Abdul, his pace unabated. "They are our mounts." The ott with the rider flapped its wings a few times and took to the air, over the buildings and out of sight. "They have been out gathering information, and the reports they bring back are not good." The captain spoke in a dark, despondent tone. "Our situation is dire. We are vastly outnumbered by the forces outside our walls. The men and women of this city have changed. They have lost hope and do not get along well, not even with one another. We will not be able to hold off a goblin attack. The majority of the guards and many of the knights have deserted, leaving us to fend for ourselves. I am down to only a handful of able bodies, of whom I would not number among the brave, and I fear they will give way with the slightest intimidation from the goblins. If I had half a mind, I would have left as well."

Haniah felt her stomach drop as he spoke. He was not the optimistic and heroic leader she had been hoping to find once they reached the safety of the castle. It was apparent that the hearts of men had failed even here in the capital of Gathbiyya.

They climbed an impressive flight of stone steps to a large cobbled plaza that looked over the city and the wilderness abroad. At the top of the stairs toward the front of the plaza, there stood a large bronze statue. Behind the statue, across more cobbled space, the magnificent castle towered over them. "Here we are. If there is a location where the Golden Gem would be revealed, this would be it." Abdul looked up at the statue.

"Who is that?" asked Haniah. The statue was of a man with handsome eyes and a neatly trimmed beard.

"That is the late King Alim. It was his wife, Queen Anwar, who gave her life to bring about the magic gems that saved his life and, ultimately, the kingdom." He paused to wring his hands. "Now, where is this Golden Gem that is supposed to save us?" He turned to look toward the dark goblin camp over the city wall.

"Well, we don't exactly know," said Ghali sheepishly. "We have the Green Gem, the Blue Gem, and the White Gem." He and Haniah held the gems in their hands to show him.

"Where is the Red Gem?" asked Abdul as he turned to look at them, scorn etching his face.

"It's been taken—"

"Captain Abdul!" The words came from a knight who was quickly climbing the stairs.

"Just a moment." Abdul excused himself to meet with the fast approaching knight, his purple cape flowing behind him.

"That statue looks exactly like my father," said Haniah softly, once the captain had moved out of hearing range. "What would a statue with my father's likeness be doing here?" Puzzled, she looked to Ghali.

"You say the statue resembles your father?" The Elver placed his chin between a thoughtful finger and his thumb. "It may very well be that the late king is a relative of yours."

"My relative?" Haniah's mouth dropped open. "Me, related to a king? I don't think so. I come from the West Hills, and my father is a farmer."

"The royalty of this kingdom has Elver blood in it. The Queen Anwar, his wife, was Elver." Ghali continued to think. "I have seen how you wield the sword. Your agility could be because of Elver blood." The comment made Haniah think. It would explain her father's superhuman sense of smell, and how her father had sensed something on the wind the night they were attacked. It would also explain how he was able to see such great distances.

"Wait. Let's not get ahead of ourselves," she told herself as much as Ghali. "I don't have pointed ears."

"The logic is sound. It is at least reasonable to speculate that you, Haniah, might have royal blood." He paused to observe Haniah's reaction. She looked at him, searching for answers. "If you were to ask my opinion, I think you would make a good princess."

"A princess?" Haniah gasped. She ran anxious fingers through her hair. "I used to think I knew what it would be like to be a princess. Fine clothes, crowns, no chores." She looked into Ghali's eyes. "I *can't* be royalty. Royalty has not only their own lives to think about, but the lives of all the people in their kingdom. They have to place their own needs to the side and make important decisions that affect others. I can't do that. I do not want to be a princess or a queen or any kind of royalty. And I don't want anything to do with the threat that stands outside the city walls." She pointed a desperate finger toward the goblin army. Black clouds now loomed beyond the dark horizon.

"It's okay, Haniah," said Ghali, placing an arm around his friend to calm her. "You don't have to be anything you don't want to be."

"The goblins that had chased you here have all gone back to their camp," said Abdul as he came back to where Haniah and Ghali where standing. "My scouts have informed me that they are now making preparations to attack the city. The guard here will show you to a place where you can be cleaned and get some food. You will need your strength in the coming hours."

The guard led them to a room in the castle where a small meal was placed upon a simple wooden table. He handed Haniah a change of clothing. "In there is a tub filled with water." He pointed to a doorway leading to a second room.

"Thank you" replied Haniah.

The guard and Ghali exited together.

The bath was warm and the clothes clean. Haniah felt refreshed. The soup and bread she ate at the small table filled her appetite with satisfaction. Things were becoming comfortable just as Captain Abdul interrupted her peace. "The guard has informed me that the goblins are advancing." He turned and started to run. Haniah followed. They ran through the castle up a flight of stairs to a place where Ghali stood waiting. They could see the goblin army lined up just out of archery range. Goblins with biting, foaming mouths carried swords, clubs, and shields. Behind the horde of goblins, large catapults were loaded and waiting.

At the helm of the army was the man that cast dread into Haniah's soul, the man that had taken her family. His black cape waved in the subtle breeze. He was carried out to the clearing on a tower, hoisted on the backs of a hundred goblins. The procession moved forward like a massive beast. High above the ground, with the gem-topped staff in his hand and his arms stretched wide, the wizard spoke.

"Give me the girl and the gems, and I will let you live." The wizard's menacing voice was amplified by the magic emanating from the Red Gem. His words could be heard all over the city.

"Who is he?" asked Ghali.

"The wizard, Amjad Fatih," answered Abdul over his shoulder. "He was once one of the king's most trusted advisors and sat on the king's council."

"What happened?"

"Eleven summers ago, there was an assassination attempt on the King and his pregnant wife. Because of the danger to the King and his family, they went into hiding. After the King left, Amjad Fatih desired to abolish the King's council and take control of the kingdom himself. The other council members exiled him from the kingdom. Now he is back with an army, and it appears he has the Red Gem of Anwar." Abdul stopped to take a deep breath. He turned to speak to a guard standing nearby. "Send message to the traitor, we will not be heeding his call." The guard turned and quickly moved off the wall.

"You're not going to turn me over?" asked Haniah, relieved.

"I am not yet so heartless that I would turn over a young girl to that evil wizard. We will fight."

Haniah frowned, wishing there was an alternative. "Can't we negotiate with him?" she asked.

"We will see," said Abdul.

They watched as the guard left the safety of the city walls and walked out upon the plains to speak with the wizard. He stopped before the towering pile of snarling flesh Fatih stood upon. Far out of hearing range, Haniah could see the guard gesture with his hands as he delivered his message. Rage surged through Fatih's face and body. With one wave of his staff, the messenger fell dead to the ground. A deafening roar sounded from the goblin horde, and they immediately set out at full charge toward the castle.

"Sound the alarm!" yelled Abdul. The cry of a high pitched bell rang out from within the city walls. "Looks like he isn't interested in working things out," he said to Haniah. "Guards, take courage!" Soldiers ran frantically to their posts. Some ran to the top of the wall with bows drawn and swords unsheathed. Others ran to fortify the heavy gate far below. Knights ran to their mounts in the stable yard and took to the air aboard the ott flyers. Everywhere the bell sounded, frantic action took place to anticipate the realization of their fears. "Get down!" Abdul yelled when he noticed a large fire ball hurtling through the air toward them.

Haniah ducked behind a short wall next to the walkway as the enflamed projectile struck the wall, causing it to buckle and shake. Catching herself with her hands, she stood back up to peer once more over the wall. The goblin army moved forward and had closed the gap between them and the city. Thousands of goblins climbed the city wall. Hundreds more of the snarling black creatures pressed themselves against the city gate, threatening to break it open. Behind the swath of goblins, others launched fiery missiles from giant catapults. Above, ott flyers raced to engage a black, snake-like mass of grocks that twisted and turned in unison around the oncoming knights.

Abdul hastily led them down a flight of stairs to the courtyard below. A blast of rock and rubble showered them from above. Haniah looked up to see that the part of the wall where they had just been standing was no longer there. In its place was a gaping hole, and a flood of goblins poured in, swinging clubs and gnashing their teeth.

"Your sword is needed," Abdul said to Haniah. "Stay and defend the castle." Turning from her, he ran toward the stable up the road.

"Where are you going?" she called.

"I must get to the skies!" he yelled over his shoulder.

Ghali pulled back on his bow and let go a volley of arrows of white light in the direction of the majority of the goblins. On the wall, guards fought for their lives, but were being overrun by the evil creatures. Ghali's arrows bought time for some and saved the lives of others, allowing them to fight on. But most could not be saved as the melee overtook them.

The great wood door that was keeping the city from being consumed was struck full force by a battering ram from the other side. It exploded into a million splinters. Haniah ducked to avoid being hit by shrapnel.

"Fall back to the castle plaza!" yelled Ghali to the fighting guards. Still firing arrows, he took a few steps back and spoke to Haniah. "We need to get to higher ground." Ghali covered the retreating guards as they ran through the streets, up the steps to the castle plaza.

The battle became more balanced as a hundred ascending goblins fell to archers' arrows. The few who made it to the top of the steps fought against an equal number of guards wielding steel swords. "We can make a stand here!" said Ghali with a cheer of encouragement.

In the sky, the fighting Gathbiyyans had no such rally point. Vastly outnumbered, each ott rider desperately fended for themselves against three times their number. A knight swung her sword at one grock, only to have a second and third ram into her from behind, knocking the rider from her perch and sending a blast of ott feathers into the air. Their claws and teeth dug deep into the ott's flesh, sending it spiraling out of the sky.

Another ott flyer with a wounded knight landed in the midst of the battle on the castle plaza. Haniah helped soften the rider's fall as he slumped and fell to the ground. "Help!" Haniah yelled, holding pressure to his wounds until two guards came to carry him into the castle.

"What do you think you're doing?" asked a shocked Ghali. Haniah was climbing onto the back of the now riderless ott.

"I'm going to fight!" she exclaimed, drawing her sword above her head and digging her heels into the ott's sides. With a burst of energy, the ott flew into the air. By the time Ghali could scream that she didn't know how to ride an ott, she was out of hearing and charging the nearest cluster of grocks she could find. Sword arm outstretched, she pointed her glistening spear toward the black mass of danger. "For Barir!" she exclaimed through the emotion that swelled and churned within her chest.

She sliced through the first and second grock at tremendous speed, sending them tumbling to the ground. The third flew by too quickly, and she missed. She twisted her head around to watch it dive out of sight. Before she could get her head back around, a fourth grock hit her square in the chest and knocked the wind out of her, nearly throwing her off the back of the ott. The grock's gnashing teeth snapped inches from her face. She brought her hand under its chin and pushed the heavy head away from her. She brought her sword hand around and beat its nose with the hilt of her sword. The fighting grock repositioned its grip and swung around to the ott's underside. The grock's claws wrapped around the ott's neck, and tried to pull it down. It hung heavy on the ott, like a lead weight. Disoriented, Haniah pulled on the ott's reigns in an attempt to find some balance. She could no longer see the blue sky above or the ground below, only flurries of darkness around them, and Haniah struggled to keep the ott in the air.

A pair of grocks buried their claws into the ott's wings, one on each side. The ott struggled to get away but was no longer able to fly. A sudden sense of dread hit Haniah as she realized she had overreached and gotten herself into a situation that neither she nor the ott could get out of. Just as the grocks threatened to crash Haniah and the ott, a great gust of winter wind blew in. The grocks released their grasp as their wings froze over. With a blizzard of snow and ice, the three grocks were sent hurling away from Haniah and her steed. Haniah's ott flapped its freed wings and flew higher.

"Only warm hearts can withstand my fury!" said a booming, familiar voice.

Haniah took courage when she saw the owner of the voice. Flying in amidst the clamor of grocks was a magnificent silver dragon with its wings outstretched. "Shudun!" exclaimed Haniah. "What are you doing here?"

"Madam Nuwairah sent for me." A group of grocks swooped in to attack. The dragon took a deep breath. His great lungs filled with summer air, and he extended his neck, letting loose a frozen breath. The dragon's breath was nothing like what Haniah had expected to see. Instead of fire, Shudun shot out a frozen breath colder than any winter wind. The grocks' wings iced over, making it impossible for them to fly. Now harmless, they dropped from the sky. "She said you could use my help."

"That I can," she said with a smile.

Darting through the flock of grocks, Shudun took little time in thinning the group of flyers down to a manageable number.

"Follow me!" Haniah turned the ott toward the city below with the dragon in tow. Above the city wall, the dragon soared and let down a frigid storm of wind and snow, leaving a large swath of ice-covered goblins in his wake. Upon seeing their frozen counterparts, the remaining goblins didn't know if they should fight harder or retreat. Ghali's men advanced with their newfound advantage and pushed the goblins back. The unfrozen grocks still flying above moved back to the goblin camp outside the city walls. "That's it! We have 'em on the run, Shudun!"

Haniah flew up and circled the castle spires before alighting upon the tallest of them. The remaining guards on the ground were few and the knights on ott flyers even fewer. There was still a large number of goblins, and the battle within the city raged on. Seeing how much damage the dragon had done to the goblin ranks and what he continued to do, Haniah began to hope.

∽⌥

Standing high upon the bent backs of goblins, the wizard surveyed the events out on the plains. He raised his staff and began to speak softly. Dark clouds from the east rolled in on bellowing winds. His voice grew as the enchantment strengthened. The Red Gem glowed and silent bands of lightning began to flicker from one thundercloud to another.

Out on the plains and high in the air, the wind grew in strength, making it difficult for anything with wings to fly. The otts that were able to land did so quickly, the others struggled until they fell from the sky. A great whirlwind created a funnel cloud where Shudun was flying. The turbulent wind beat against his body, making it impossible to maintain control. The more he struggled to fly, the more effort the wizard put into his enchantment, until finally Shudun was forced to land where he was, out in the open between the city and the goblin camp.

Haniah watched as she saw the horde of goblins overpower Shudun using nets and ropes. He fought as well as he could, but his advantage was in the air. Once on the ground, they jumped on him, kicking and biting. Without the advantage of flight, and being vastly outnumbered and undersized, it did not take long to subdue him. Haniah closed her eyes in frustration, not knowing what she could do. There *was* nothing she could do. One lone rider on one lone ott attacking an army of goblins and grocks would be suicide. So she hung her head, unable to watch the capture of the regal dragon.

The clouds blocked out the sun as the day turned gloomy. The goblins below captured the castle plaza, overtaking Ghali and the guards defending it. Ghali was mobbed by a dozen goblins and bound with ropes.

A clap of thunder and streaks of lightning exploded in the city, sending sparks and flames hurling into the sky. Black bellows of smoke floated up to the sky, letting all know the siege had breached the city walls, and there was no one to save it.

A purposefully placed lightning bolt struck the tower Haniah sat upon. The deafening crash of thunder and the accompanying flash rendered her blind and left a painful ringing in her ears. The ott instinctively leapt to an adjacent spire with Haniah still on its back. It clung to the tower's slippery tiles with its front claws. Seeing white, Haniah blinked rapidly to regain her sight. Black dots formed in her vision as she rubbed her eyes. The blurry, black dots grew bigger and clearerer very quickly, forming into the remaining grocks. And they were approaching fast. A flair of panic shot through Haniah's body.

"We have to get out of here," she said, nudging her heels into the ott's ribs and sending it into a dive toward the castle below, hoping to gain speed.

The grocks quickly pursued her as she flew around great white pillars and shingled roofs. Her brown curls whipped in the air. Several grocks veered off and made their way around a spire to cut her off. Leaning hard right and then left, she dodged the grocks attempting to block her path only to run into more at every turn. Unable to keep up with the quick twists and turns, Haniah sent her ott barreling through a great stained glass window high above the army below. Broken glass went flying in every direction as Haniah tumbled into a room decorated with marble and onto a floor covered in an ornate, crimson rug.

She got up quickly and climbed back on her ott, then charged through a second stained glass window set at the other end of the room and out into the open air. "Keep it up!" she said, patting the ott encouragingly on the neck. "You're bleeding." Haniah held up a hand smeared with blood to her face. She could feel the animal strain, panting heavily as it struggled to continue. They flew to the west, toward the safety of a grove of trees. "We can make it!" Haniah looked back at the distant grocks. "Hurry!" she said, giving encouragement.

Haniah and the ott crashed into the thick cover of trees. Haniah ducked as leaf covered branches whipped at her face. The ott labored to gain control. On the ground she hid near a bush and looked up at the canopy of limbs above. The ott lay unmoving on twig-covered dirt next to her. Amid the silent trees, she held her breath. Her pounding heart was a stark contrast to the stillness of the grove. There, she lay, waiting for them to find her and take her.

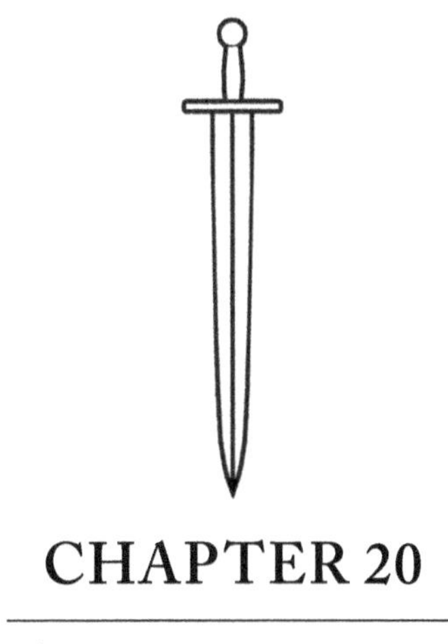

CHAPTER 20

The Sword

HANIAH SHUFFLED HER FEET AS SHE WALKED WEST ALONG THE Gold Road. Dejected, destitute, and depressed, Haniah limped with her head down, shoulders rounded. She kicked a stone here and a pebble there.

Behind her, and far in the distance, vestiges of smoke lingered from the previous day's battle.

She had hidden in the trees overnight after bandaging the wounds of the ott she had escaped on. It was tired and unable to carry its rider anymore, so she let it go. She had asked enough of the poor creature.

The sun had returned, but the usual warmth and comfort that came with a new day did not. She thought about the loss of her family, her friends, the kingdom, and the home in the West Hills that would never exist again. A comfortable bed, a loving smile from her father, something yummy made by her mother—all were memories that would now remain just that, memories. Any hope of restoring these things were lost with the fall of Gathbiyya. She had only one gem left in her possession. Her quest had come to a dismal end.

In her gloom, she did not notice the wind sweeping over the field, bending tall grass as it approached. A second and stronger gust blew her hair over her face. Dust from the road swirled in a turbulent spiral. She raised her arm to shield her eyes from the loose debris. When the wind settled, she lowered her hands and opened her eyes. Madam Nuwairah was standing before her, skirt rippling in the now gentle breeze, staff in hand.

"Hello, Haniah," came her sweet, soothing whisper of a voice.

"Where did you come from?" asked Haniah, giving a half-interested response.

"I hope there will be time for answers someday, but now is not the time," said Nuwairah. "You must turn back. You're going in the wrong direction."

"Wrong direction?" Haniah scoffed at the woman's comment. "No, there is nothing I can do back there."

"If you do not go back, all will be lost. You are a guardian of the gem."

Haniah stared past the wizardess, off into the distance, not listening to a word the woman spoke. Seeing that she was not getting through to her, Nuwairah stopped speaking and moved to look her in the eye. "How does your leg feel?"

"It hurts." A tear ran down her cheek. Her heart was in so much pain, it felt like it would burst. Nuwairah waited, letting Haniah display her feelings through a few more tears. After wiping her face, she looked at Nuwairah with puzzled eyes. "How do you know about my leg?"

"I have my ways. The important thing right now is not to decipher how I do what I do. The important thing is for *you* to carry on." She nudged Haniah's shoulder with the top of her staff, encouraging her to stand up straight. "Show strength."

"I have no strength. I am weak."

"Show courage," she said, pounding the point of her staff into the ground. "I believe you have it in you. Do not let your friends' lives be given in vain."

"I can't!" In frustration, Haniah cut the woman off. "I can't do it! All is lost! Did you not see what happened?" Haniah pointed an angry finger back in the direction of Gathbiyya.

"If not you, then who?" asked the wizardess in a respectful tone.

"How about nobody!" Her words came out sharp. "What about the hero in the woods? The one I saw on the night my family was attacked. Maybe he can do something. You know, the hero you sent. The one that killed Barir and nearly killed me. Or how about you?" she asked accusingly. "Why don't you try doing something about it, if you want something done?"

Nuwairah paused and spoke with a calm voice, her hand extended. "Let me see the gem." Haniah pulled the White Gem from her satchel and handed it unceremoniously to the woman. "Stand close. I want to show you something."

The wizardess reached out and Haniah felt a shock at the woman's touch. Immediately they were whisked away into a spiral of flashing color and dropped into complete blackness. She could feel Nuwairah's hand on her shoulder as her eyes adjusted to the abrupt change in lighting. Shapes and shadows of tall trees slowly formed around her. "Where are we?"

"Not only where are we, but when are we?"

"When are we?" Haniah mouthed the words to herself in contemplation. She looked up to the sky and noted that no stars were shining. She looked for the three stars that reminded her of her family, but they were also missing. "Where are the stars that shone over there?" she asked, pointing in the direction they had previously been.

"They have yet to appear." said Nuwairah "Please, speak softly. We are very near your family's farm on the night they were attacked."

"Wait a moment," said Haniah, trying to understand the significance of what the woman was saying. "You're telling me we have gone back in time?"

"Precisely." The woman gathered her skirt up around her. "Now if you will please stay here, there is something I need to attend to." The woman stepped over a branch to walk away.

"Wait," Haniah whispered with alarm. Nuwairah paused. "You want me to stay here? In the dark? Alone?"

"Yes." With that, the wizardess turned and walked away into the night.

Alone in the dark, her mind began to ponder as she looked around for something familiar. The trees were tall, they looked like they could be the trees in the West Hills. Where did the wizardess go? What could the woman be up to, and what was she supposed to be doing herself? She had followed the woman's advice before, and it had caused her nothing but hardship. As these thoughts went through her mind, a great explosion erupted in the forest, throwing a ball of fire into the air and her onto the ground.

Through distant trees, Haniah could see the home she had grown up in fill with flames. Flickering orange light was reflected in the small glints in her eye. Tall slits of light were cast between the trees, and they created long, dark shadows across the forest floor.

The silhouette of a fleeing person came toward Haniah from the house, followed by additional shadows. The grunts and snarls from the chasers let Haniah know that goblins were pursuing. Without hesitation, Haniah tightened her grip on her sword and set out at a run in their direction. Leaping into the air, she brought the hilt of her sword down on a goblin that had just tackled the fallen runner, causing his victim to fall to the ground. With all her dexterity, determination, and desire, she struck down one goblin after another until they were either laying lifeless on the ground or fleeing from her as fast as their ugly, frightened legs could carry them.

Breathing heavily, her sword pointed defensively in front of her, she circled, looking for any additional threats. When she could see none, she lowered her eyes to the person who lay unconscious on the forest floor. In the dim light, she could now make out the form on the ground. It was no stranger she had saved, it was herself.

"I remember the first time I looked upon myself," said Nuwairah, stepping out from behind a tree, the White Gem on the top of her staff giving a faint, but illuminating glow to the area. "It can be a little surreal."

"That…that's me," stammered Haniah, pointing to herself lying on the ground.

"Yes it is," said the woman. "What I need you to do is to go to your home and find something to eat."

"Find something to eat?" asked Haniah, bewildered by the request.

"Yes, if I remember correctly, your mother has a cake on top of the stove." Haniah stood staring at the woman, wondering whether she was serious. "Don't worry, there is no danger there now, and I have not destroyed everything." Haniah still stood, stunned. "Move along. Tap, tap." She gently waved her hand to move the girl along. "And something to drink as well," she called once Haniah began to move toward the house.

The explosion had blown off the roof and the fire had gutted the house, leaving the dark sky above and only burnt remnants of what used to be there. A few small flames remained, giving a little light to see by.

Stepping into the doorway, Haniah noticed the charred kitchen table where her family once sat and where her father first showed her the map leading to the gems. That time felt like seasons ago. So much had happened between then and now. She would never have believed back then all the stories she could now tell. Broken chairs lay smoldering on the floor. In the dark, she stepped on something. Bending down to pick it up, she realized it was the small toy horse her father had carved for Najid. The toy reminded her of how alone she felt and how she actually missed the way her brother would say "bish" when trying to say the word "fish". Sticking it halfway into her pocket, she walked to where the kitchen had been, to the cast iron pan sitting on top of the stove. Lifting the lid, she found a perfectly baked cinnamon cake, lightly toasted on the edges, somehow magically preserved from the destruction all around. After searching the floor around her, she picked up a little wooden bowl and placed a piece of cake inside. After tying down the lid, she reached into a blown out cupboard, grabbed a metal flask, filled it with milk that had been brought in earlier that day, and returned to the woman waiting in the woods.

"Who are you exactly?" asked Haniah, handing the items to Nuwairah.

"I am your father's assistant and a member of the king's council," she said, giving a straight and honest answer. "Before your father took your mother and family away, he used to live in the capital of Gathbiyya. He sought a safe place to raise his family, away from the big city and the spotlight. He wished to find somewhere safe, away from anyone who would seek to harm him or those he loved."

"Is my father the king then?" asked Haniah, looking at the crest on the hem of the woman's clothes.

"Yes, he is," answered the woman in the affirmative.

"And who would want to cause harm to him?"

"Your father, the king, sat upon the throne when there was an assassination attempt upon his life. A witheram attacked him from the shadows. In the ensuing struggle, your father escaped unharmed, but the assailant got away. At the time, the conspirators were unknown. Because of the uncertainty of your father's would-be assassinator, your family went into hiding in the West Hills." Haniah listened intently to the story. "Your mother was pregnant at the time."

"With me?" asked Haniah.

"Yes, with you." She nodded her head. "To ensure his own safety and the safety of his wife and unborn child, no one was to know where he had fled. Not even me. So, I cast a spell on myself, erasing my knowledge of where he had gone. I was tasked to contact the king only upon threat of death."

"What does that mean? Threat of death?" she asked.

"I was not to have located your father unless there was a threat to his and his family's lives," she continued. "Through my investigation, I discovered that a fellow council member, Amjad Fatih, had been the one who ordered the assassination upon your father's life. I, along with others loyal to the king, confronted Amjad and ran him out of the kingdom. Over the summer, I discovered Amjad had stolen the Red Gem of Anwar and was on his way to kill your family in an attempt to gain a second."

"That is why you came to us on that night," said Haniah. "To warn us?"

"Yes."

"That was you who visited us during supper?"

"Yes." The woman smiled, remembering. "A younger version of myself. If I recall correctly, the memory spell I had cast on myself was wearing off. I may have been a little out of sorts that night. Nevertheless, it was I who turned Amjad away this evening, with the aid of the White Gem."

"So, you're strong enough to fight him?" asked Haniah.

"That was Amjad a season ago," said the wizardess, shaking her head. "If I were to face the Amjad from our time, he would be much more powerful. Not only does he have the Red Gem, but now he has the Green and the Blue as well. Someone with more power than I must face him now. That is why I must give the gem back to you." She took the gem from off the top of her staff and held it out for Haniah to take.

"No, I can't. I have no powers," Haniah protested. "You have magic like he does, and the White Gem makes your magic stronger."

"What is needed is something more powerful than magic." She spoke with authority. "True, I have hope. Hope in a young girl. That hope has gotten me this far and has even helped you. But you have courage, selflessness, and a pure heart. You have the qualities needed to defeat the darkness, and those qualities are more powerful than magic. You have shown you can wield the sword, but now you must show you can wield the gem."

"But I already had the gem. It did not help me when I needed it."

"Well then, think about that," she said smartly. "Who says you need it then? You did this." She waved her hands over the goblins strewn around on the ground. "You did this without the White Gem. You have faced goblins and countless other fears without the White Gem. Now, imagine yourself with it. As we practice our abilities, they grow. Your courage has grown and your sword skills have improved as you have exercised them and put them to use." Haniah thought about what the woman was saying. "To see a person as they are in a single moment is like trying to view the entirety of the world through a pin hole. Who you were then is different than the person you are now. And the person you will be tomorrow will be different than the person you are today." She paused to lean in, placing her weight on her staff. "What you have seen is a mirror of sorts. Can you see what you have become and what you might become? You're no longer the frightened little girl you once were." She gestured to the young girl lying on the forest floor. Haniah looked at herself, her brown curls resting on a bed of ferns. "Look at her. There *she* is, and here *you* are. The hero!"

"I am the hero!" repeated Haniah. "Then who was it that killed Barir?"

"One of Amjad's minions, a specter called Death."

"And her?" asked Haniah speaking of her past self, still lying unconscious on the ground. "What will we do with her?"

"I'll wait with her until she wakes." The wizardess looked at the concern on Haniah's face. "She will be okay." Bending down, she picked up a satchel that lay next to the fallen Haniah and placed the cinnamon cake, the milk, and Najid's toy horse within.

"When she awakens," said Haniah, "tell her to drink deeply. It will give her strength."

"I will," said the wizardess. "Take this." She handed Haniah the White Gem. The warm feelings of comfort, courage, and acuteness all returned to Haniah. "I can get you to where you need to be without it. I am much better at moving forward than I am at going back." With those words, Nuwairah gave a wave of her staff, and Haniah was gone.

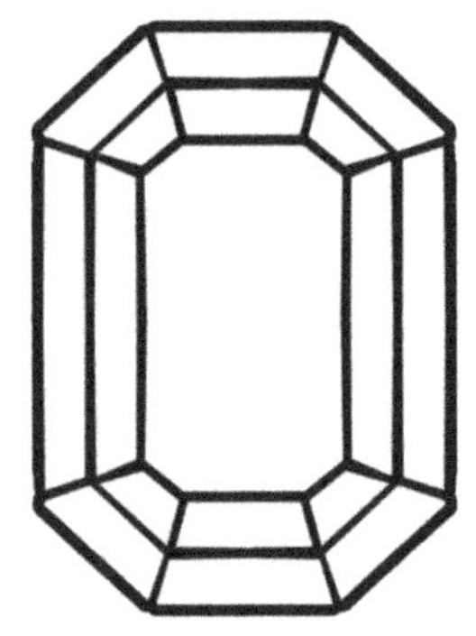

CHAPTER 21

The Gem

Black smoke smoldered above the burnt out city. Grocks soared high above in a victorious formation. Goblins searched for survivors, dragging them out of their homes and into the streets. Fathers were ripped from their families and were shackled and marched to the castle plaza. Children were taken from their mothers and locked away in large iron cages, crying in terror. Mothers screamed and fought helplessly to save their little ones.

On the plaza terrace, encircled by a throng of gurgling monsters, Amjad Fatih stood in judgment of a bound and chained Ghali. Tired and beaten, Ghali knelt before the black robes of the evil wizard, the Blue, Green, and Red Gems sparkling on top of his staff.

Haniah took the long staircase up to the hard, flat stones of the castle plaza. "Let him go," she said, walking boldly through the mass of salivating, mud-covered creatures encircling the terrace.

"Have you come to die?" asked the wizard sardonically, raising his sinister head from Ghali to give Haniah his most evil grin.

"I have come to meet my fate." Haniah looked into his eyes and could see there was no feeling there, no mercy and no hope, only darkness.

"Yes, that is well. I will grant you the opportunity now to beg that I kill you quickly."

"Haniah!" Ghali fell silent as the wizard pointed a twisting finger in his direction. He bent over in pain. Haniah moved to help her friend stand, his feet shackled and hands bound.

"You're helpless in saving your friend. I have more strength than you could ever hope to have." The wizard jabbed his finger at Ghali again, sending him into convulsions. "Once he is dead, I will squash you like the bug that you are."

"You are strong, and by comparison, it may appear we are weak," said Haniah, holding Ghali. "You have taken my family from me, and now you have hurt my friend. I will trade you the White Gem if you let him go."

"No, don't do it!" cried Ghali

"I'll make that trade." Amjad gave a swift wave of his staff, causing the shackles that held Ghali to loosen and drop to the ground.

Ghali's muscles relaxed. Haniah released her hold on him and let him stand on his own. Haniah knew that to attack the wizard with her sword would be futile, leading to bitter and angry feelings within herself. "I cannot always change things to the way I would like them to be. I accept that. But what victories I can get I will take."

She broadened her stance and firmly placed her feet under her. She spoke confidently. "You may win, but you do not have power over me or my friend. Because this is *my* choice." She reached into her satchel and pulled from it the shimmering White Gem. "I give the gem to you and I give myself to what is meant to be. I will not use violence."

The wizard motioned the onlooking witheram to retrieve the gem. With a greedy grin, the witheram handed the gem to its master and slinked back among the crowd of onlooking goblins and grocks.

"I have won, and my army will now govern the land," said Amjad, placing the White Gem on the top of his staff. He raised his arms to the sky. The gems glowed red, blue, green, and white. "I shall reign with terror and blood."

"I wouldn't say you have won just yet," said Haniah.

The world groaned and the ground heaved. Stone from the castle and the surrounding buildings began to break. Haniah reached out her hand to brace herself from the shaking ground. An enormous cloud moved between the world and the sun, eclipsing its light and turning the day to night. She peered through the dark and saw the three faint stars of her family flicker far in the distance.

"Bow down and serve me! The darkness has won."

"The Golden Gem will be revealed!" gasped Ghali. Haniah looked to him and winked.

Amjad looked to the sky and shook a clenched hand. "The Golden Gem will be mine! I am in possession of all four gems."

"You may be in possession of them, but you were not rightfully given the gems. Only one with a pure heart can weild the true power of the Golden Gem." Haniah folded her arms, proud to fight the way Barir would have fought.

Amidst the turmoil, darkness, and destruction, Haniah could feel a warmth begin to grow in her chest. Inexplicable feelings of comfort and joy flooded her. An unseen force swirled around her, blowing through her dress, stirring the curls on her head and lifting her into the air. Her arms became lighter and her toes pointed down as she hovered a pace above the ground. Warm feelings turned to energy and illuminated her skin. Radiant streams of light shone from her finger tips and escaped as a thousand beams of light from the ends of her hair. She dropped her sword. She was a shining beacon, providing light to the entire city.

"The Golden Gem!" said Ghali, rising from the ground to look at Haniah who was still floating in the air. A warm gold light illuminated her skin. Emotions of hope, peace, and love radiate from her.

Everyone in the kingdom saw her actions. They witnessed her bravery in standing up to evil, they saw her selflessness when giving herself up in hopes of freeing her friend, they saw her love for her family, and now they saw her light, the pure heart she was. The warmth from her actions moved the hearts of all those watching. Each individual felt warmth in their chest. It started small, but gradually grew and moved out to their extremities, lifting their spirits and giving them hope. The goblins and grocks, unable to handle such feelings began to glow with the heat of an oven. Many hid their faces, cowering and huddling, while others turned to flee then burst into flames. The flames and smoke died in the wind coming from Haniah. The monsters were nowhere to be seen.

The bands on the imprisoned people of Gathbiyya were loosened and the bonds of the chained burst.

The witheram ran to Amjad, clawing at his robes and begging to be hidden. In an effort to stop the feelings, Amjad raised his staff and struck out with all his power, might, and magic at his enemy. The ray of evil shot like a bolt of lightning from the wizard's staff, but it was absorbed by the halo of light permeating from the Golden Gem. Unable to control the flow of his emotions, the wizard's attack backfired, burning him and the witheram to a crisp husk. The charcoal remnants of the two stood for a moment, but were soon blown away by the wind emanating from Haniah. The four gems situated at the top of what was once a staff fell to the floor.

The three distant stars moved down from the sky, growing larger and brighter until they gently touched upon the ground.

Haniah slowly lowered her feet to the pavement, the light in her countenance subsided, the wind now gently swirling.

The cloud blocking the sun rolled away like a stone moved from a darkened tomb, bringing natural light to the world once again.

Haniah's family crossed the plaza toward her on foot. She ran to fall into the open arms of her mother and father. Her brother, Najid, was brought into the middle of the hug by his father's broad reach. Together, they embraced.

"We are so proud of you," said her mother, pulling back slightly and extending her arms to look into Haniah's happy face. She wiped the tears from her daughter's cheeks.

"You're so brave!" exclaimed Najid, refusing to let go of his sister.

"You mean you saw me?"

"We saw you, Haniah. We saw it all," said her father. "We have watched you from above throughout your journey. We cheered for you when you escaped the wolves; we cried with you when you lost your friend." He tightened his embrace. "We have been with you, and you with us. You gave us hope to hold on. Now, we are here, together." He let out a sigh of joy and relief.

Throughout the kingdom, families and friends reunited. Mothers kissed their children. Husbands loved their wives, and siblings embraced.

∾ ∿

Haniah ran her hand over the words, "Blue to soothe the soul in time of sadness" inscribed on a portion of the plaque at the base of a towering statue. It had been erected on the castle plaza next to the statue of King Alim, the husband of Anwar. Together, the two statues looked out over the vast view of the kingdom. The burned down buildings had been rebuilt, the broken glass fixed. Families had returned to their homes.

The faint twinkling lights of the long lost stars began to show in the early evening light of dusk. With the return of the stars came an addition to the night sky Haniah had not seen before, a star in the north.

"Barir, you were the first to help me on my quest, the first pure heart I came across. You helped soothe my sadness." She looked up at the polished bronze nose on the face of what looked like a bear statue. At least, that's what she had thought he looked like when she first saw him. Now, looking at the statue, she no longer saw an animal, but true humanity.

Haniah heard the rustle of slippers on the stone floor behind her and turned to see a Huggar woman with a child in her arms walking toward her.

"I am sorry—" Haniah started.

"You have no need to say sorry. You did all you could. Your father, Fadi, told us what happened. I wish to pay my respects and to thank you." She looked up at the statue. "I am grateful he was with a friend when he passed."

Haniah looked tenderly upon the little child in the Huggar's arms, a child she knew would now grow up without a father.

"This is Bakri," said the Huggar woman. The child smiled.

"I can see his father in his deep eyes. He will probably be a thinker like him."

"That may be the case," the mother said with little passion.

"He did have a message for you," said Haniah reverently. The woman holding the child nodded her head, indicating she was ready to hear it. "Well, it's actually a message for you and your son." A lump formed in her throat. "He said to tell his son and wife that he loved you." The Huggar mother gave a solemn smile, keeping her emotions checked.

"Thank you," replied the Huggar. "I am sure the message will bring my child comfort when he is older." Haniah could see the heartache behind the Huggar woman's loving embrace of Barir's child.

"I am sorry," said Haniah in an attempt to bring some comfort.

"Like I said, there is no need to apologize." She bowed her head. "Now, if you will please excuse us."

"Yes, of course," said Haniah as the woman turned and left. She watched them descend the long staircase.

"I see the staff of Anwar has been bestowed upon you." Haniah turned around to face the speaker. She watched the wizardess, Nuwairah, approach from the other direction. Haniah looked down at the crystal scepter she held in the crux of her arm. "That is the very staff Anwar held during the battle of Mt. Hashalah and at her death. It is very powerful and can only be carried by royalty."

"Yes, it is a very nice staff." She ran her hand across its smooth surface and stared longingly back up to the statue of her friend, Barir.

The wizardess turned her gaze upon the plaque fastened to the statue's base and read it out loud.

"To the Golden Gem it is given
White to light the way in darkness
Blue to soothe the soul in time of sadness
Green to grow courage true
Red to burn the hearts anew"

"The prophecy has been fulfilled."

"What do you mean?" asked Haniah.

"The gems do not refer to stones alone. It also refers to people," explained the woman. "You are the Golden Gem. To you, each of these blessings has been given." She pointed to the words on the statue.

"If I am the Golden Gem, then this prophecy is not only about me, is it?"

"No, it is not. It speaks of people you know, and the gifts each have given you."

"Then it must be speaking about you as well," she added, "You're the White Gem. You lit my way in the darkness."

"Yes, I guess it was a very dark night when we first met." She leaned on her own staff, reminiscing. "You have come a long way from being the frightened little girl I once knew. Instead of being frightened of the dark, you now embrace your emotions and approach the world with a new view. You will make a wonderful princess."

Nuwairah and Haniah both turned their heads to the approaching guard who had ascended the steps and now moved to stand before them. Haniah gestured for the captain of the winged guard to speak.

"The dwarf has been found and captured. He is now here," said Abdul. Haniah looked past the knight. A few steps from the top stood a short, raggedly dressed dwarf encircled by guards.

"Bring him to me," she said.

"As you wish." Abdul motioned with his gauntleted hand for the others to bring the prisoner forward.

Haniah recognized the face of Hadi, the guide who had led them to the Stairs of Jabal and betrayed them on the ice-covered mountains of Hayud. Upon seeing Haniah, he removed his hat and threw himself to the ground, his knees and forehead touching the stone floor.

"I'm sorry." His voice quivered. "It was wrong of me to steal." He looked up at the likeness of Barir. "It is because of me your friend is dead. They used me to find you." He put his face in his hands and cried. "They took the money. I cannot repay you. I can do nothing to make up for the wrong I have done you and your friend." The dwarf continued to cry.

"Your emotion shows your heart," Haniah said. "I do not need a magic compass to show me that. I can see that you are sorry and that your heart has changed." The dwarf looked up at Haniah, not fully understanding what he was hearing. "Your crimes have already caused enough hurt, and because of your repentance, I will not condemn you. I forgive you and offer you an opportunity to serve the kingdom."

"What kind of service would you wish me to perform?" asked Hadi, willing to do anything that might help make the situation better.

"Whatever you're capable of," said Haniah. "The duration of that service I commend to your own judgement. You are free to go."

"Free to go?" he repeated, not believing what he heard. He looked around at the guards and back to Haniah. He spoke softly and humbly. "Thank you!"

"Please stand," said Haniah.

Hadi rose to his feet and gave three continuous bows with his head. "Thank you. Thank you! I won't disappoint you." He shuffled his feet backward to the steps where he turned and began his journey home, the guards following. Neither Haniah nor Nuwairah said anything until the guards were out of sight. Silence hung in the air.

"Well, I think your heart is in the right place as well," said Nuwairah after watching the interaction. "It takes a special person to forgive as you did. It is this, as well as all your other good attributes, that make you the gem that you are." The woman gave Haniah a hug, knowing that what she had done was not easy.

"There is one more matter of business," said the wizardess, pulling from her sleeve an old envelope colored with age. "I looked over the castle's archives and came across this letter written many seasons ago." She handed it to Haniah. "You should take a look at it when you get a moment. When I found it, it was enchanted with a spell of protection and hidden within the pages of a book. I have looked it over and find the message to be authentic."

"What is it?" Haniah turned the envelope over to see a royal seal.

"It is addressed to you. It appears to be a new adventure for a subject who resides within the kingdom." Haniah gave her a quizzical look, but the woman did not say any more on the matter. She motioned for Haniah to move along. "The council is waiting in the throne room." Haniah placed the envelope in her pocket and turned from her dear friend.

The great doors to the castle opened onto a grand hall decorated with stained glass, marble walls, and magnificent tapestries. She walked down an aisle lined with familiar and unfamiliar faces, all dressed in their nicest and most formal clothing, reserved for only the most prestigious occasions. At one end of the room was the magnificently carved doors Haniah had just walked through. At the other end was a dais where a royal Golden throne sat vacant.

Haniah walked halfway down the long hall, stopped, and turned to the side. There among the crowd of onlookers was Shudun the dragon. "Barir died as the guardian of the Blue Gem," she said, turning to the dragon. "He helped soothe my soul in times of sadness when I was missing my family. His death has taught me how to embrace my emotions. He showed that one does not need to use violence to get what they want. Now I ask if you, in his absence, will once again be the guardian of the Blue Gem."

"I would be honored to hold the title of guardian once again," said Shudun. Haniah reached into the satchel she carried over her shoulder and pulled from it the Blue Gem. She handed it to the dragon who accepted it gracefully.

"You have taught me that I can be strong and still be sensitive." Haniah gave him a smile of gratitude. She then moved further down the line to where Ghali stood.

Haniah addressed him. "Ghali, guardian of the Green Gem. You have shown courage through trying times. Your example in standing up for what you believe even when it was not popular to your people or your family has brought me courage. You are not what they said you are. You are not a deserter, but a loyal friend. Thank you." Haniah nodded her head to extend her thanks and he returned the gesture with a deep bow and a tip of his hat.

"Father," said Haniah, speaking as she moved to stand before the dais. "Will you once again be a guardian by accepting the Red Gem of Anwar?"

"Yes, I will," he said. Haniah pulled from her satchel the Red Gem and handed it to Fadi.

"The Red Gem has truly burned hearts anew. No longer are the people of the kingdom callous, selfish, and cold like they once were. The Red Gem has also burned my desires anew," said Haniah. Her father raised an eyebrow at her, questioning. "I no longer have the desire to be royalty. I am happy being me. I am happy with the life I have always had. With you."

"You are the perfect candidate to become royalty *because* you no longer care to be royalty. And that is also why you are called to the position." He took her hand in his and helped her up to stand on the dais. "It is those who want the power who abuse it. Those who do not seek it are the ones who should receive it."

Her father turned her around to face the crowd. Standing in front of the throne, Haniah looked out at the different faces in the throng of invitees.

"The council recognizes you as being worthy of royalty," said Ghali, coming to stand before her. He held a plush pillow on which a royal crown rested. It was made of fine metals, rubies, and diamonds and was so ornate and beautiful that, only a season ago, it would have left her dazzled. "It is customary for the princess to be presented to the people wearing the crown of Anwar. At your request, the crown of Anwar will rest next to the throne." Ghali moved to stand to the side of the dais.

"Haniah," said her father coming to stand on the dais with her. "As King of Gathbiyya and the ruler of the West Kingdom, I confirm upon you the title Princess Haniah of Gathbiyya. I give to you all the rights and power pertaining to this royal position." He took the moment to look on her with pride. "As your father, I find you worthy of royalty." He pulled a wreath made of white daisies from behind his back. She bowed her head, and he placed it on top of her curly brown hair. "May you always be blessed, as are all those who know you."

Embracing her father, Haniah threw her arms around his neck and squeezed. When she let go, he gently wiped a tear from his eye and turned to the crowd. "I present to you my daughter, Princess Haniah of Gathbiyya, Princess of the West Kingdom." Her father stepped down from the dais and the people welcomed her with an uproarious applause that filled the room and echoed throughout the castle.

The cheer poured out of the castle doors and into the plaza, down the streets and into the countryside, along the Gold Road, across the West Hills of Aini, and past an ancient well. The applause sounded in the ears of a ground moose in the Shahirah Forest and in the ears of a giant red fox. The triumphant sound soared to the heights of the frozen mountains of Hayud, through an abandoned Huggar fortress and to the south, past a sacred grave in an orange-walled canyon.

The kingdom was changed. The applause that echoed throughout the land was from those who were now kind and pure in heart. Theirs was a place of joy and peace. For so blessed was the West Kingdom with the coming forth of the Golden Gem, they never again were threatened with darkness.

THE END

The following pages have been taken from a larger
composition of drawings. Created by the hand of
Fadi, on parchment, following the
arrival of the Golden Gem.
They are submitted as historical documents
along with the manuscript "The Golden Gem"
to the royal archives of Gathbiyya.
Witnessed by myself,

Nuwairah,

First Wizardess of the Three Circles.

FADI'S SKETCHBOOK

FADI'S SKETCHBOOK

FADI'S SKETCHBOOK

FADI'S SKETCHBOOK

Nathan and the Crystal Scepter

THE STRANGE HAPPENINGS OF THE STRANGEST DAY OF NATHAN'S life did not begin when he received a video message from himself. A video he did not remember making. A video telling him to hide.

No, the strange happenings began earlier in the morning when he saw a very hairy person riding on the bus with him. He noticed the hairy man's eyes peeking over the collar of his long coat as though he was trying hard not to be noticed. The hat on his head towered at least a head taller than everyone else. But it was the large, blue, hairy hand holding the railing overhead that first caught his interest. When Nathan looked up at the giant person, the stranger turned his eyes away, shielding his face with his shoulder.

In spite of trying to hide behind his coat and hat, part of the stranger's face was clearly visible to Nathan for just a moment. He saw a face covered in short, neatly-combed hair and a black, glossy nose. For a second he thought it was a bear, but it couldn't be a bear, because bears don't ride city busses at 6 am.

The fur was blue. He had never seen a bear with blue fur. Nathan leaned forward in his seat to see if he could get a better view without drawing attention to himself. It was a balancing act he performed for just a moment before realizing that he wasn't going to get a better view than the one he had already.

The stranger kept his back toward Nathan with his face staring out the window. A set of furry ears with tufts of blue fur on the ends stuck out from under his hat. They twitched with every jostle of the bus.

Outside, the streets of Seattle passed by. Street lights glistened off the wet ground and the tall building windows reflected the gray clouds above. The sun had not fully risen and provided only dim, solemn lighting to the city.

Nathan had started eating the second of his three Oreo cookies when he first noticed the tall man … er, thing. Nathan couldn't wait until noon and had gotten the Oreos from out of the lunch his father had packed for him a little earlier that morning. Nathan reached into the clear Ziplock bag and pulled out the last cookie. "Would you like a cookie?" asked Nathan tentatively as he reached out and touched the creature's coat sleeve with the hand that held the cookie. With a grunt, the thing moved its free arm away from Nathan's outstretched hand and placed it on the bar above, next to his other hand, blocking Nathan and the rest of the crowded occupants from getting a better look at him.

Teetering on the edge of his aisle seat, Nathan leaned forward just as the bus applied its brakes, and he quickly grabbed hold of the seat in front of him. A couple people stood and moved to the doors of the bus.

The bear-like person leaned over to where Nathan sat, his large head looming close. The breath from the thing's nostrils blew through Nathan's hair. It spoke. "Stay safe," came a deep, soft rumble that buzzed like a bee's nest. It was soft enough for only Nathan to hear.

Once the doors opened, the people exited, followed by the giant, blue man in the hat and rain coat. Nathan's jaw dropped as he watched the beast exit out on the street. For a beast it was. He saw its beastly eyes and large, white teeth as it leaned in. Nathan was so startled that he hardly realized when the monster had gone.

The bus began with a jolt. Nathan kept his eyes on the creature standing on the side of the street until the bus pulled away and the blue stranger was too far away to see through the misty rain.

"Nathan, grab your backpack," Nathan's father said. "Ours is the next stop."

"Did you see that dad?" asked Nathan.

"See what?" His nose had been in work email for the entire bus ride.

Nathan looked back to where the bus had stopped, but could not see the beast. "It was just here on the bus."

"Lots of things to see on the bus," his father said distractedly. "Grab your things."

Nathan placed his hand on the backpack he had sitting between his legs. Had he just seen a bear? Maybe a trained bear. Maybe the circus was in town and one of their bears escaped. But no, that sounded preposterous, even to someone as creative and open-minded as Nathan. Maybe it's a person with some kind of birth defect. He had seen pictures in books where people had super long fingernails and hairy feet. It must have been someone like that.

Nathan rubbed his eyes to test if they were working right. It could also be that it was too early in the morning and he had yet to fully wake up. 6 am was earlier than when he normally woke up. Today, Nathan was going with his dad to work. "It's take-your-kid-to-work day," his dad had informed him a few days ago. Nathan had been excited to see what his dad did for work and to see where he spent his days. But now he was pre-occupied by the beast, and exactly what it meant when it said, "Stay safe."

Regardless of the reason for the beast's cryptic words, Nathan had just seen a real, live monster on the bus. That was when the strangeness began.

Acknowledgements

Like any epic fantasy you first must have a band of adventurous heroes. So has been the case with the creation of this book.

I wish to thank my sister-in-law Melinda, an avid reader of all things fantastic who was the first to read the manuscript and lend her skills as an editor.

Thank you to Lily, Carter, JJ, Ryan, and Hannah for reading early copies and giving me the confidence to send my writings to a publisher. You're the middle grade audience I hoped to reach.

Special thanks to Heather Godfrey my editor who tirelessly worked on making this book the magical read that it is.

Thank you to Kirk Edwards and the team at Snowy Peaks Media who saw the great value in publishing a book like Haniah and the Golden Gem. A book that can instill a sense of courage, resiliency, and imagination within a young audience.

About the Author

JASON FORD LIVES WITH HIS FAMILY IN BEAUTIFUL EUGENE, OREGON. He enjoys music, sushi, bicycling and spending time with his wife, Kristen, and their two kids. There is a little bit of Jason in all of his characters. Yes, even the evil ones, but especially the good ones.